HIS OWN MAD DEMONS:
DARK TALES FROM DAVID A. RILEY

Parallel Universe Publications

First Published in 2012 by Hazardous Press
This edition Parallel Universe Publications 2015
Copyright © 2012, 2015 David A. Riley

Lock-In was first published in *The Black Book of Horror*, Mortbury Press, 2007

The Worst of all Possible Places was first published in *Houses on the Borderland*, BFS, 2008

The Fragile Mask on his Face was first published in *Dark Discoveries #15*, 2009

Their Own Mad Demons was first published in *The Fifth Black Book of Horror*, Mortbury Press, 2009

The True Spirit was first published in *Back from the Dead*, Noose & Gibbet Press, 2010

ISBN: 978-0-9574535-8-6
Parallel Universe Publications, 130 Union Road,
Oswaldtwistle, Lancashire, BB5 3DR, UK

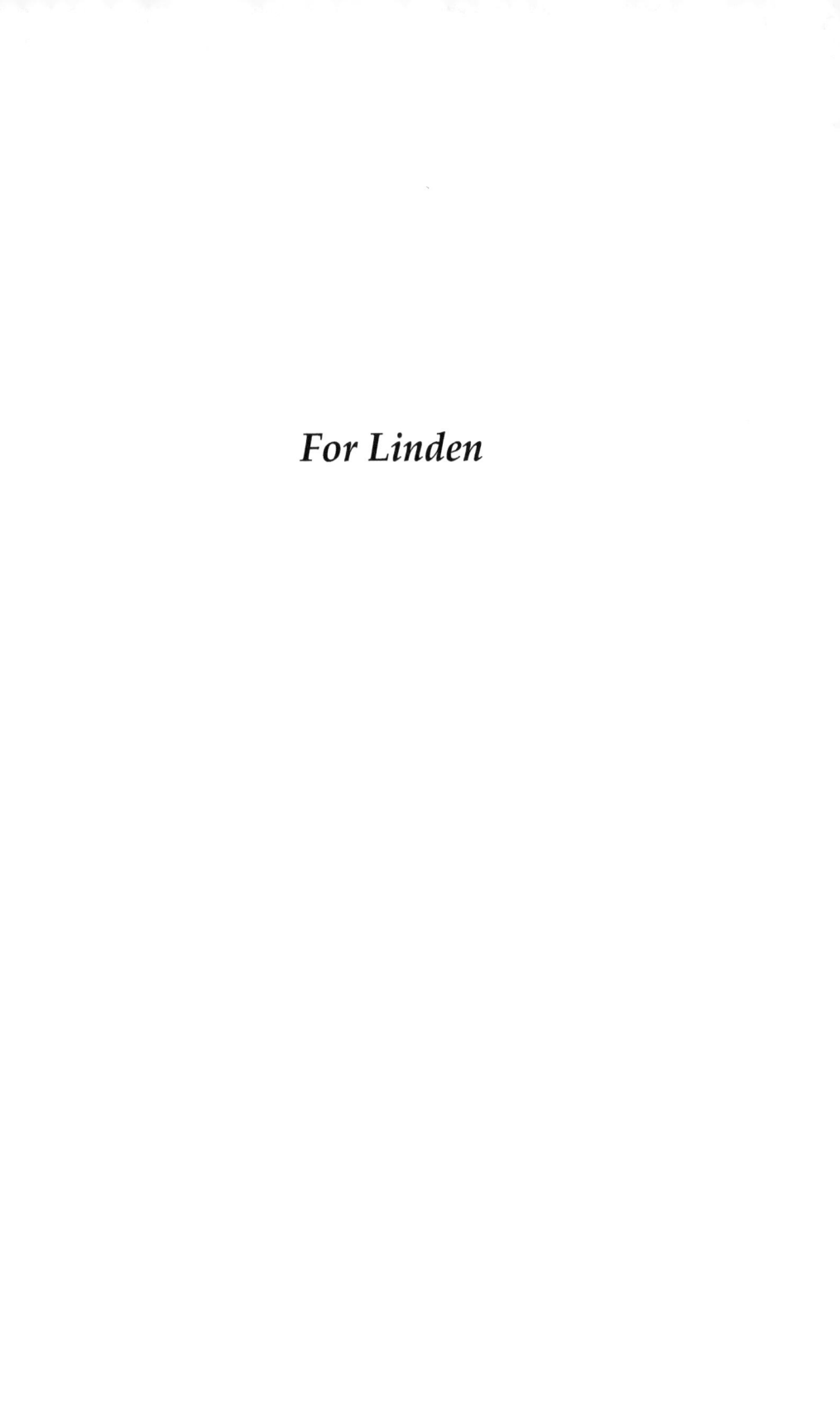

For Linden

CONTENTS

THEIR OWN MAD DEMONS

Nobby pulled up by the canal in his transit van. Rain swept across the road and forced the few trees along the tow path to sag beneath its onslaught. A dull headache from the eight pints of beer he drank last night in the Bell and Compasses hurt his eyes as he switched off the wipers. Instantly the depressing scene was hidden as rain beaded the windscreen. A couple of moments later the passenger door was tugged open and Stinko Parkinson pulled himself in.

"Filthy friggin' 'orrible weather," the old man spluttered, shaking the hood of his parka - a parka so greasy Nobby was surprised the rain hadn't simply slithered from it instead of soaking in.

"Worse thing is, you dirty old bugger, we can't even open the bleedin' window to let in some air. Soddin' Hell, Stinko, don't you ever have a bath?" Nobby smirked. At six feet three and a good twenty years younger than Stinko, he couldn't care less how much he upset the man.

"Where're we off to?" Stinko asked between puffs, as Nobby kicked the van into gear and manoeuvred it down a short stretch of muddy potholes back to the main road.

"What d'you care, so long as you get paid for it?" Nobby swore as the van stalled. He restarted it with quick, jerky movements.

"It's about time you got yourself a decent van. Look well if it lets us down when we can't afford it to."

"I'll worry about that. It's never let us down yet, has it?"

"Yet!" Stinko laughed. "There's a first time for everythin'. The way this thing's actin' it won't be long afore it packs in for good."

As the van lurched onto the road, Nobby's lips twisted from his teeth. The filthy old bugger was starting to get under his skin. One word more and he'd lamp him, he thought. Good and proper. He glanced at him sideways. And wished he hadn't, as his nose was filled with the sour smell of unwashed clothes and stale urine that surrounded the man. Despite the rain Nobby lowered the side window a couple of inches and breathed in the air that blew, rain-flecked, at his face.

"What're you tryin' to do, friggin' well freeze us to death?"

"If you didn't stink so much I wouldn't need to." Nobby pressed down hard on the accelerator and the van bounced faster down the road, overtaking a Mini which he forced maliciously towards the kerb. "Get out of my way, you stupid cow!" he shouted at the driver, a suddenly sallow faced woman who swerved even more to avoid his bumper.

Ten minutes later they pulled up at a junk yard. Piles of cars loomed over its corrugated iron fencing. A sign above its open gates read:

Joseph Burger & Co
Scrap Metal Merchant

Joe Burger himself, as fat beneath his flashy pale grey suit as an oil-rich Arab, stood by the prefabricated office near the gates, talking to one of his younger - and dimmer - employees on how he wanted his wine-red Mercedes, parked nearby, cleaning and polishing, his stubby arms waving instructions. Seeing the Transit van he frowned, dismissed the young lad with a nod of his head, then strolled self importantly over, hands in his pockets.

Nobby climbed out to greet him.

"Never mind the niceties," Burger silenced him. "I've a job for you and your smelly friend. Come into the office. Stinko can wait in the yard. I'll leave it for you to explain the details to him later."

"Righto, Mr Burger. Okay," Nobby jabbered. "Whatever you say."

"Exactly." Joe Burger led him into the office. "Sit down." Seating himself behind the desk that dominated most of the room, Burger reached inside one of its drawers and took out a gun. It clunked heavily as he dropped it on the desk. "It's loaded. Four rounds. Though with any luck you'll not need them."

Nobby stared at the revolver, his thin face pale.

"You've used one before?" Burger asked.

Nobby shrugged. "Once," he said, reluctantly. "A few years back."

Burger laughed. "No need to be shy. You'd be surprised how much I know about you. I make a point of finding out as much as I can about my employees, especially those who can be relied on to carry out *special* tasks."

"You wouldn't be wantin' me to kill someone for you, would you?"

Burger laughed again. "If I wanted someone killing I wouldn't ask you. The gun is for your protection. An insurance, if you like. A dissuader. Something to stop those I want you to meet with some stuff from getting too greedy and thinking they can have the cake and the ha'penny. Though it's not a cake we're talking about. And it's a damn sight more than a ha'penny too." The fat man leaned back in his chair till it creaked and his sparse but shiny, well-groomed hair touched the wall behind him. "You've heard of the Gortons?"

Nobby scratched his ear. "Sure, Mr Burger. Hard nuts. One of them was doing time when I got sent down a few years back. Big headed bastard. Bloody well ran the prison. Or thought he did."

"He probably did," Burger said, "if half I've heard about them is true."

"Is it them I'm meetin'?"

"It isn't Mickey Mouse. I'd hardly be talking about them now if there wasn't a point, would I?" Burger retorted.

Nobby stayed silent, though he wished one day, when he didn't want the greaseball's money so much, he could meet him somewhere nice and quiet where he could get on with kicking his balls into pulp without interruption. The picture in his mind of Burger's blubbery lips dripping blood as he begged for mercy, helped to keep Nobby's face from showing too much resentment.

"I want you to go to this address." Burger passed him a slip of paper. "Pick up the stuff that's handed to you and take it to the second address. There you should be handed a parcel of money. There'll be twenty K in it. In fifties. Check it. And don't get any funny ideas about scarpering. You're neither clever nor fast enough." He patted the gun. "I've more than this I can lay my hands on. And others who would like nothing better than a chance to sort you out."

Nobby shook his head. "You needn't have any worries about that, Mr Burger. What you pay me's enough."

"So it should be," Burger added, bluntly. "There's an extra five hundred in it for you and your friend. For the risks. Though there aren't that many. The Gortons are a bad bunch to do business with, but they're not stupid. They'll know I've taken precautions."

Nobby glanced at the gun, unsure how serious Burger was. The gun looked old, and there was rust on the barrel. And although he had used a gun before, that was eight years ago when a sawn-off shotgun he'd been given by Biffer Tompkins went off by accident at a sub-post office in Endon, shattering a display of Kinder eggs and putting the wind up Biffer, who legged it for all he was worth. Nobby had only gotten away by sheer luck. In the stunned silence that followed the blast a stupid old git of an OAP had snatched at the gun. He'd squawked when the barrel burnt his fingers and caused enough confusion, as he jigged about nursing his injuries, for Nobby to dash outside, jump in the van they'd left by the corner and drive off as fast as he could. Biffer had been less fortunate. Racing across a road two blocks away, he was stupid enough to run in front of a passing police car, rolled across its bonnet and concussed himself on the road, earning himself two weeks in hospital and seven years in Walton, with time off for good behaviour. Just how much of this Burger had found out, he didn't know. What he did know was that guns were a lot less reliable than most people thought.

Reluctantly he picked up the revolver. He stowed it in his overcoat, then went on to pick up the paper as well.

"When d'you want us to meet 'em?" he asked.

"In two hours time. It's all been arranged. Just make sure you keep your eyes skinned." Burger smiled as he rose to his feet. "Come back with the money and I'll pay you out."

Nodding his head, Nobby walked from the office and back to the van.

"I don't friggin' like it." Slumped like a wrinkled heap of misery beside him, Stinko stared at the rain still lashing itself across the windscreen. "I don't friggin' like it at all."

Regretting having told the old man about the gun, Nobby shrugged as he drove down the road, only minutes away from their rendezvous with the Gortons, the five large cardboard boxes they'd collected slowly swaying in the back of the van.

"It's too late to worry about that," Nobby said. "We're almost there."

Stinko snorted. "If I'd known what kind of job we'd be gettin' I wouldn't've come. I've heard o' them Gortons. They're a bad lot. They wouldn't think twice o' doin' us over and takin' the lot, van and all."

"Just let 'em try." Nobby patted the gun in his pocket.

"Pah! And what d'you think you'd do? Pretend you were John Wayne? I know what you'd bloody well do, you soft pillock. You'd have more chance of shootin' your own friggin' foot than one o' them Gortons, especially if they've shooters o' their own, which the bastards friggin' well will have, mark my words." He picked out a shred of tobacco that had stuck to his tongue from his roll-up. "Yon gun that fat Yid gave you will probably blow up in your friggin' face anyway, if you're daft enough to fire it."

"Fuck you!" Nobby's lips twisted, baring his teeth, in a mixture of anger and nervousness.

Stinko smiled. "Say that to the Gortons when they're bustin' your legs for a bit o' fun."

Mouthing a response, Nobby indicated right, then drove down a short, winding road that took them between a few hundred yards of dismal-looking fields, before arriving at a boarded-up redbrick office block at the entrance to a quarry. Not used for years, the quarry's walls rose towards a fringe of grass high above. Behind the building, hidden from the road, Nobby saw a large grey car and a pickup van. A group of men stood, sheltering from the rain, inside the open door into the building.

Nobby drew up a few yards from them, leaving the engine in neutral as he turned to Stinko.

"Hop out and open the doors so they can see what we've brought."

Two of the men strode towards them. One of them, his thinning hair plastered to his scalp by the rain, jerked a thumb towards the back of the van.

"Check them out for us, Joey," he said to the other man. His broad smile, twisted beneath a misshapen nose, had a worrying lack of humour. Instinctively Nobby touched the gun in his pocket, moving his fingers around it. The man's face was hard. Too fuckin' hard.

"You got the cash for us?" Nobby called from the van.

"It's here." The man opened his coat and pulled out a brown paper parcel.

What spit still remained in his mouth drying up, Nobby said: "Mr Burger told me to check it first afore we handed anythin' over."

"He did, did he?" The man's smile broadened humourlessly. "Would you like to climb out and check it?"

Nobby glanced at the men stood inside the building. They were watching intently.

"Well?" the man asked.

Nobby shrugged. A heavy, debilitating tension coiled inside his stomach. His fingers slid around the gun. "I can check it just as well in here," he said.

"You can fucking well check it outside," the man grated. His brittle eyes stared straight at Nobby's. "Do you know who you're talking to?"

"I - I were told by Mr Burger - "

"And who the fuck cares what Burger says? You can tell him from me that Reggie Gorton lays down the rules, not Joseph fucking shit-face Burger. When I deal with people I expect them to act with respect. Not treat me as if I was no more than a back street barrow boy." The man's fake smile reappeared. "Are we going to finish this properly? With respect? Or are you going to stay in that van as if you didn't trust me?"

Nobby glanced at the men still stood inside the office block.

The other man, Joey, returned with Stinko.

"The stuff's okay," Joey said. A razor scar puckered his cheek as he grinned. "This old bugger don't half pong, though. Burger'll be hiring bag ladies next as receptionists for his fucking scrap yard."

Nobby glanced at Stinko, who was shuffling his feet in agitation. His eyes looked scared. And Nobby wondered if Joey had said something to him while they were at the back at the van.

Undecided, Nobby half pulled the gun from his pocket. He didn't like the place they were at. He didn't like its isolation. And he didn't like how many of Gorton's men were hanging around.

What was that fat Kike up to messing around with people like this? Reggie Gorton was known to be a friggin' psycho, who'd had more bodies put away over the years than anyone else in the city. And never been nailed by the police either, even though everyone knew about him.

Nobby turned as the rest of the men strolled towards them, positioning themselves in front of the van.

Reggie Gorton cocked an enquiring glance at Nobby. "Are you getting out or not? I haven't all day to piss around in the rain."

"Okay," Nobby said. "I'll take the parcel. I don't need to check it. I trust you."

"That's big of you. That's fucking well big of you indeed, my friend." Reggie turned to his men, grinning. "I like that," he grated. His grin undiminished, he jerked the van door open. "Get out and do what your boss told you." He thrust the parcel into Nobby's arms. "Count it. Here."

Releasing his hand from the gun, Nobby dropped to the

13

ground. Rain splashed across his face as he grasped the parcel, his fingers shaking so much he almost dropped it.

"Alright, Mr Gorton." His fingers fumbled with the edges of the paper as he ripped it open.

A click made him pause and could feel his balls crawl into his groin. A sawn-off, double-barrelled shotgun, no more than three feet away, was pointed at his face. A sour taste filled his mouth as he stared at the end of its barrels. Holding the gun, Joey grinned as the parcel fell from Nobby's hands. Instinctively Nobby snatched at it, his mouth gaping when he saw the sheets of newspaper that scattered across the ground.

Reggie laughed. For the first time there was a hint of humour in it, as behind him Stinko moaned sickly.

"Good lads," Reggie said. He strode towards Nobby, patting him on the back. "It's good to see Burger's not improved with age. Still too tight to hire anyone better than a pair of deadbeats to do his dirty work." Reggie turned to his men. "Get that stuff shifted. And carefully. Some of it's fragile."

Joey waved his gun to the left. "Over there, string-bean," he said to Nobby. He nodded his head towards the office block. "Both of you. *Shift!*"

He followed behind as the men reluctantly made their way towards the building.

"What're you gonna do to us?" Stinko asked in a pathetic whine which even Nobby couldn't help but despise. ""You're not gonna hurt us, are you?"

Joey laughed. "You shouldn't take no notice of what you've heard about us. We don't go in for things like that. Not to people who behave themselves and do as they're told," he added, prodding Nobby in the middle of the back with the shotgun. "Even though some buggers sometimes try their best to get up our noses."

Nobby stumbled as they went inside the office block. Its mildewed, graffiti covered walls were cracked from neglect, and scabs of plaster lay across the concrete floor. Broken doors hung from their hinges, giving glimpses of deserted corridors and empty rooms. Leaks through the roof had left puddles on the floor. Dodging them, the men crossed the room, Joey behind on their heels.

"That's far enough," he said at last. "Sit by the wall." Obviously enjoying himself, the gangster waved the shotgun from side to side, emphasizing the seriousness of his order.

His lower lip trembling, Stinko sidled down till he was crouched on the floor. His hands in his pockets, Nobby stared uncertainly about the room. It smelt of death.

"I told you to sit down," Joey repeated.

"And then?" Nobby asked.

"If you behave yourselves, nothing. If you don't..." Joey flexed his finger on the trigger. "There's room enough to hide a body or two in this place."

Stinko tugged at Nobby's coat. "Do as he says, you daft bugger. Can't you see he means it?"

Joey nodded. "And I do," he said, smiling, the razor scar shining on his cheek.

Putting his back against the wall, Nobby slid to the cold, concrete floor, though his fingers were already tight around the gun in his pocket. Its barrel was aimed at Joey's stomach, not ten feet away, unsure even now why he knew he had to do it. Somehow, for some reason, he knew neither he nor Stinko were going to get out of here, no matter how obedient they were. Once they'd done everything Joey told them to do he'd shoot them.

Nobby's fingers curled around the trigger in his pocket, slowly, carefully, his heart beating faster till he was sure he would have a coronary if it didn't slow down soon. His face felt flushed as beads of sweat dribbled from his hair.

"You look as if you're about to shit yourself," Joey said with a smirk. "You don't trust me, do you, string bean?" Balancing the barrel of the gun in one hand, he pointed it at Nobby's head with a nonchalance as frightening as it was false. Nobby's fingers tightened on the gun in his pocket. In his imagination he could already hear the shotgun blast that would scatter his head in a stew of brains, bones and blood across the wall behind him.

"So help me," Nobby started to mutter, his thin lips trembling with tension as his finger pulled one millimetre more on the trigger in his pocket. His coat ripped forwards as the gun exploded, bursting a blackened, smoking hole through the cloth as it spurted out fragments of charred fabric through the air.

Joey's face jerked forwards in a violent nod as he was thrown back, doubled, his gun going off reflexively as it whipped skywards, blowing a yard wide, almost circular hole through the ceiling. Mewling, he rolled over and cracked his head on the ground, his legs twitching. A deep-throated, hideous moan gurgled from his mouth as his hands clutched at the blood on what remained of his stomach.

Nobby jumped to his feet. He grabbed hold of Stinko and shook him.

"Come on! We have to get out of here before the bastards get us. They don't know who's been blasted yet. They'll think it was us. But it won't be long before they realise it wasn't."

Stinko stared at the man on the floor. "Why d'you do it?" His voice sounded desperate. "They'd have let us go after they'd taken the stuff."

"And maybe not," Nobby muttered. "You know these Gortons. They're mad bastards. I did what I had to do. Let's get out of here while we can. We've no other choice. Unless you want to see what kind of thanks Reggie Gorton'll give you."

"After what you've done, you daft bugger, they'd kill me."

"Then you'd better get a move on, hadn't you?"

A quick glance through the doorway showed they had no hope of escaping that way. Their van was too near the other vehicles, all of which were surrounded by Gorton's men, two of them carrying one of the cardboard boxes to their pickup. Reggie Gorton was staring at the building, drawn by the gun blasts, and seemed on the point of coming over to check things himself. Nobby knew they had only seconds to get out of here.

"Come on. Quick!" he told Stinko. He strode past Joey, still mewling like a cat that had been run over by a car. Ignoring him, Nobby pushed through a door onto a long corridor flanked by

16

more doors, all of them shut. At the far end a sharp bend led to an empty warehouse. Broken windows lined its outer walls, too high for them to reach. At the far end, next to a steel, roll-up door, was a smaller one made of wood. There was a narrow strip of light down one side of it.

"It's open," Nobby said. "Come on."

"Half a mo' there, Nobby. I'm not as young as you. I need a second to catch my breath." Stinko's feet stumbled, his bristly face mottled with purple blotches. His lips looked blue. "You're killin' me," he panted.

Nobby grabbed at his arm, gripping it hard as he tugged him along.

"If we don't hurry, Reggie Gorton'll be killing you for real, you daft old sod."

Already they could hear shouts echoing through the building behind them as if from a great distance away, though Nobby knew better. He tugged at the door. It sprang open and slammed against the wall. Outside they could see the road leading out of the quarry past fields turned a misty grey in the rain. None of the Gortons were in sight. Probably they were all in the office block now, Nobby thought, some of them seeing to the man he'd shot, while the rest would be starting to search the buildings, looking for them.

"Back to the van," Nobby said. "If we can get to it before they find us we'll get away from them."

Stinko shook his head. "We'll never get away from them. They'll hunt us down wherever we go after what you did, Nobby. We'll never get away. Not for good, we won't. You've doomed us, you bastard. You've doomed us both."

Nobby took hold of his collar. "Quit your whining. We'll get out of here."

Throwing the man to one side, Nobby dashed through the rain. Skidding to a halt at the edge of the building, he peered around the corner. Satisfied, he called Stinko on.

"They must have gone inside. Now's our chance."

The noise of the rain helped drown the sound of their feet as they ran to the van, Stinko wheezing and coughing behind him. Reaching it first, Nobby was relieved to find the keys were still in the ignition.

"Get in!" he urged, not waiting till Stinko was in his seat before starting the van up. The engine growled into life, backfiring twice. With a snarled: "*Shit!*" Nobby slammed the gears into first and the van lurched forwards.

As they drove off, one of the Gortons ran out of the office block brandishing a shotgun. Nobby thought it was probably the one that Joey had threatened them with, as the man was still trying to reload it by the time the van was well on its way to the open gateway out of the quarry. There was a bang, and a handful of pellets beat a half-hearted tattoo against the rear doors, shattering one of the windows, then the van was bouncing along the road.

"Look out!" Stinko shouted.

Too late Nobby tugged at the steering wheel in a desperate attempt to veer the van away from the ditch beside the lane. But the front wheel had already spun into it, jamming in the sudden dip and dragging the rest of the van sideways in a drunken skid. The steering wheel was whipped from Nobby's hands, almost dislocating his wrists. Cursing at the pain, he grabbed at the wheel, but the van had already tilted too far. Realising it would end up lying on its side if he let it move forward, its chassis screaming alarmingly, he slammed on the brakes. A violent shudder rippled through the vehicle.

"*Nooo!*" Stinko whined, his hands to his face as he cringed back as far as he could in his seat.

The vehicle creaked as it lurched back and forth, half of it overhanging the ditch.

Peeling his hands from his face, Stinko peered through the windscreen. Nobby grimaced. His mouth tasted coppery and foul and his bladder was all but ready to burst. Remembering the danger they were in, he reached for the keys and tried to restart the van. The only response was a long drawn whine from the engine. He tried it again, but the whine had grown weaker, and he glanced at Stinko, a sinking feeling in his stomach.

"It's not going start, is it?" Stinko's voice sounded faint, a disheartened murmur. "The friggin' bastard's gone and given up on us, hasn't it?"

Ignoring him, Nobby reached in his pocket for the revolver. By now the Gortons would already be starting to pile into their own vehicles. It would only be seconds at the most before they came tearing through the gateway in pursuit. Not that they would have to go far to find them, Nobby thought.

"We'll have to get out of here," he said. "If we cut across the fields we can still get away."

Stinko stared through the rain that left the distances a dim blur of hills and trees on either side of the quarry.

"I can't," he murmured. "My heart won't take it. It'd kill me."

"Reggie Gorton'll kill you if you don't."

Stinko glared at him. Anger blazed in his vein-reddened eyes. "It's your fault, Nobby. You've gotten us into this. If you'd kept your head and not gone and shot that bastard back there they'd've let us go. You know that, you barn-pot, you friggin' nutter. You've gone and done for us."

Nobby grabbed him by the throat. "If you want to stay here, winging, do it. I'm off." He pushed the man back against his seat, then opened the door and leapt out of the van into the rain. His feet slithered on the wet grass as he pulled himself up out of the ditch and reached for the fence that ran along the edge of the field beyond for support.

Behind him, Stinko shuddered in the van. He looked down the road, his eyes wide with panic. Clumsier than Nobby, he pushed himself out of the van and struggled to climb out of the ditch, his gnarled hands slipping on the grass, his arms too short to reach the fence. He would have called out to Nobby for help, but the big man was already on the other side of the fence and had begun to run across the field, too far away to hear him now, even if he'd risk his own neck to come back to help.

On the road, a car skidded to a halt. Looking back, Stinko let out a yelp as he saw three men climb out of it. One of them pointed towards him. Even from here Stinko could see Reggie Gorton's face, livid with anger. Without hesitation Stinko tried to jump to the fence, his finger nails scratching at the wooden posts in a useless attempt to grab hold of them, till someone took hold of his arms.

Writhing and kicking, he was dragged up out of the ditch and back to the van.

"Nobby, you bastard, I'll get you for this," the old man shrieked as he stared at the figure looming above him. The man who had grabbed him, hauled him round. Rain splashed Stinko's face, mixing with the tears in his eyes.

"We've got one of you, at least," Reggie said, leaning over him. "We'll soon get the other, however fast the bastard runs."

"Please, Mr Gorton, it weren't me," Stinko stammered. "It were Nobby. It were him as had the gun. I didn't know nothing about it."

Reggie smiled, his false teeth artificially even. "Joey was my nephew." The man's voice was a harsh monotone - remorseless - his eyes cold. "He was family." He bent down and stretched his hand out to pat Stinko's cheek with a strained gentleness. "Even in the eyes of the law you're as guilty as your partner, whether you pulled that trigger or not. You were there." His smile faded, the mask discarded. "You'll have the pleasure of finding out some of what your partner is going to get when we catch up with him. Perhaps that will help to compensate. Though I doubt it." He nodded his head. "Take him to the farm." He glanced at Stinko, their eyes meeting. "No one will disturb us there while we get on with things."

*

Nobby ran faster and further than he had ever run in his life - faster and further than he would have ever thought possible, outdistancing even the crippling stitch which for three miles all but doubled him up. Staying low to keep himself as much out of sight as possible till he'd left the Gortons beyond too many hedgerows and trees to be seen, he kept to the countryside as much as possible, too scared to take the easier routes along any of the minor roads he passed in case the Gortons drove along them, searching for him.

Travelling across country, he headed in the direction of Amesbury, five miles to the east. An ex-Mill town filled with dreary terraced streets of local stone and corner shops twenty years out of date, it offered little hope of security, except there were at least a dozen similar backwaters he could have headed for. Too many for even the Gortons to cover in one afternoon. Or so he hoped. Though this did little to help ease his fear when he walked down its streets, his clothes drenched and his shoes all but ruined. If the Gortons didn't get him, pneumonia would if he didn't get into some dry clothes soon.

His first stop was a back-street pub across from the entrance to a closed-down mill. Choosing a side room at the far end of the grubby bar, he ordered himself a large whisky and a couple of bags of crisps.

"Do you have a phone?" he asked the landlord.

"Round the corner, by the Gents." Pursing his lips at the twenty-pound note Nobby had given him, the man ungraciously trudged away for some change.

After he'd come back, Nobby downed his drink, then searched for the phone. The whisky had at least begun to kindle a comforting imitation of heat in his stomach, which would do for the time being.

Ten minutes later he managed to get hold of Marcia Fielding. He'd lived with her on and off for the last few years, when he could put up with her seven-year-old son. And when he wasn't going out with someone else. She was a reliable standby. Or as reliable a standby as he had ever had so far.

"What's wrong?" she asked. "My supervisor said it was important. I hope it is and you've not dragged me away from my check-out for nothing. The old bitch has been watching me like a hawk for weeks." Her voice nearly always had a grumbling tone to it, which was why she was only a standby. Nobby grimaced at the phone.

"Tell your supervisor your Gran's on her deathbed if that'll satisfy her. Tell her whatever you like."

"*If* you tell me what you want first," Marcia said. "What is it? The Law?"

"Nothing like that," Nobby said. "Some bother, that's all. The police aren't involved." Not yet, he thought, wondering how the Gortons would handle the man he shot.

"Who is it you're in trouble with? That bloke you sometimes work for? Burger, is it?"

"Naw, nothing to do with him," Nobby cut in impatiently. "Can't we leave the third degree till later? I need some help."

"Why else would you ring me after - what is it, Nobby? - three weeks?" she said sarcastically.

"I've been busy. You know how it is."

"I *know* how it is all right," she said. "What do you want? Money?"

He shook his head automatically at the phone. "Naw, I've plenty of that. Enough for now."

"I'm glad to hear it." Her voice softened slightly. "What do you want?"

"I could do with somewhere to stay for a couple of nights, that's all. Just till things have cooled a bit." Or until he'd managed to arrange for somewhere safer to hole up, he added to himself.

"I suppose you could always stay with me," Marcia said, though he could hear doubt in her voice. "Where are you now?"

He told her. "Could you drive over and pick me up when you've finished work?"

"I'd have to arrange for someone to look after Peter."

"Ask your Mum. She always wants to look after him."

"Maybe."

Nobby leaned against the wall. "When can you be here?"

"Eight-thirty all right? I knock off at eight and it'll take me at least half an hour to drive all the way to Amesbury."

"That'll be fine."

"I hope so," Marcia said. "Just so long as this bother you're in doesn't get out of hand."

"No chance," he lied. "It'll blow over in a couple of days. You know how it is."

*

It was nearly nine by the time Marcia arrived, parking her ten-year-old Fiesta outside the pub while she went in to find him. By ten-thirty, after picking up a takeaway from a Chinese on the way, they were back at her flat on the outskirts of Edgebottom. It was in one of three tower blocks, with a view of the town on one side and the moors on the other.

A couple of hours later, a half bottle of gin drunk between them to wash down their takeaway, both Marcia and Nobby were asleep in her bed, Nobby too exhausted after the day's events to make more than a passing attempt at lovemaking. Even his worries about what the Gortons would do if they caught up with him had not been enough to keep him awake for long, though he'd left the gun that Burger had given him tucked away beneath his clothes on the bedside table beside him.

The bedroom was warm from the central heating radiator, its window closed against the winds that blew around the tower block, lashing it with rain. It was as secure a refuge as any that Nobby could have found at short notice - secure enough, he knew, till the Gortons found out about his link with Marcia Fielding and checked into it. By then, though, he would be well away from here - well away from Edgebottom too. Marcia's Fiesta was one reason he'd contacted her, though she did not suspect that yet. One of his last thoughts before he drifted into sleep was the hope he could be away in it long before she realised what he was after.

A clock tower somewhere far into town chimed two, unheard by either of the sleepers.

Up on the hills above Edgebottom the lights inside an isolated farmhouse still burned, though there were no eyes to see anything tonight as the gales swept by. There were sounds from within the farmhouse, though, sounds that sometimes cut through the howling of the wind, sounds which made the few sheep huddled by the dry-stone walls that crossed the hills in haphazard lines look up and bleat disconsolately.

Not long after the distant clock struck two a scream rang out from the farm. A scream even louder, shriller, more pain-wracked than any that preceded it. A scream that changed into an agonised whimper, then silence. Moments later someone laughed. It was harsh laughter. While a low intonation, too faint to be heard from outside the farm, went on and on...

Suddenly cold, Nobby woke. Shuddering all over, his skin prickled with an icy clamminess from head to foot despite the duvet that covered him. Startled, he stared into the darkness, his heart hammering. Holding himself as still as possible, he barely breathed as he listened to the winds and to Marcia's alarm clock ticking away on her side of the bed. For a moment he wondered if he'd heard someone enter the flat while he slept. Could the Gortons have gotten around to checking on people like Marcia so soon? His panicked mind rove over how they might have found out about her as he listened for something that might - just might - explain what woke him. When nothing moved for what seemed like hours he started to shift his arm from the duvet and reached through the darkness to where he remembered leaving the gun beneath his clothes. Feeling through them he closed his hand around the reassuringly heavy butt with a suppressed sigh of relief, gripping it tight.

Breathing deeply in an effort to ease the tension in his body, he suddenly frowned. Stinko? Recognising the old man's awful smell, he wondered how Stinko had found his way here. He couldn't mistake it. Stinko was not far away from him, he was sure.

Whipping the duvet from his body, Nobby rolled out of bed and padded quietly towards the door. He listened for a moment before gripping the handle. There was only stillness outside in the living room, no unusual sounds, only the wind, Marcia's

24

clock and her own deep breaths in the bed behind him.

If Stinko was here only his smell betrayed him, spreading through the air with its distinctive odour of sweat and urine.

With a sudden, silent intake of breath, Nobby flung the bedroom door wide open. Clenching the gun before him he scanned the living room. Still sensing nothing besides the smell, he reached for the light switch. The sudden glare dazzled him for an instant, but not enough to prevent him from seeing there was no one there.

Quickly, he searched the rest of the flat: Peter's bedroom, the bathroom, the passageway filled with boxes, coats and bags of rubbish that led to the outside door. There was no one, apart from Marcia's son, asleep in his bed.

Had Stinko been here and gone? Nobby was unable to understand it. He'd known the old man long enough to realise he was incapable of breaking in and getting out again without making a mess of the outside door, yet it wasn't even scratched, its lock still fastened. His smell was here, though, as strong as before. Perhaps even stronger.

What the fuckin' hell was he up to? Where the fuckin' hell had he gone?

"Stinko? Are you there?" he called in a low whisper. "Where the frig' are you hidin' yourself, you daft old bastard?"

He looked into the kitchen. Its neon light cast a harsh clarity over everything inside. Yet, here too, Stinko's smell was strong.

Too strong.

It wasn't natural. Even for Stinko, the bugger would have to be pressed up against him for it to be as strong as this.

"Come on, where are you?"

"Who are you talking to?" Marcia stood by the bedroom door, rubbing her eyes with one hand and holding onto a flimsy pink dressing gown with the other. She frowned at the gun Nobby held in front of him, too startled to be able to hide it in time. "What the fucking Hell are you doing with *that*?" Her face was pale and hard as she stared at him. "What kind of trouble are you fucking well getting me involved in, Nobby?"

He waved the gun casually. "It's not as bad as you think."

"Like fuck it isn't. Or do you always wander around in the middle of the night with a gun in your hand?"

"I could smell something odd."

"So odd you're prowling at three o'clock in the sodding morning with a gun?" Marcia sneered sarcastically. "You're going off your rocker, Nobby. You really are. They'll be locking you up in a nut-house next if you go on like this. *You smelt something odd!*"

Nobby clenched his fist, tempted to let her have a good old smack in the mouth. That'd teach the bitch to keep it shut!

"Can't you smell anything?" he asked instead, forcing his muscles to relax. If he hit her she'd scream till someone called the police. "Kind of sour and rancid?" he added. "Like old sweat?" Like Stinko, he could have told her if she'd met the man, which he knew she hadn't.

"There's no smell here. You're imagining things."

Nobby sniffed, Stinko's odour even stronger now. "It's here," he told her. "You must be able to smell it. It's friggin' awful."

"You're friggin' awful," she retorted. Ignoring the gun, Marcia crossed the room and picked up a packet of cigarettes from the arm of the sofa. Lighting one, she glanced at him sideways. "If I were you I'd see a doctor. Soon. And tomorrow you'd better see about getting yourself somewhere else to stay. I don't know what kind of trouble you're in, but you're not staying here. Not with a gun. No way, sweetheart."

She stepped back into the bedroom where she gathered up his clothes and dumped them on the floor outside. "I expect you to have gone by the time I get up," she said. With no further comment she shut the bedroom door on him.

Nobby stared at it for a moment, his emotions uncertain. A vein pulsed on his temple as he clenched his jaws, grinding his teeth. At any other time, at any other time at all, if he hadn't had the Gortons on his back, he'd have forced his way back into the bedroom and sorted her out good and proper. Instead, after a minute in which he forced himself to try and calm down, he started to get dressed. He'd teach her one lesson at least: by the time the bitch got up in the morning he'd be away from here in her car. There'd be sod all she could do about it. He'd already seen her keys, left where she tossed them when they arrived back earlier with their takeaway, in a glass bowl on the imitation beech wood unit by the door.

His repressed anger almost made him forget the smell. But it was too strong to be ignored for long. Stinko was here somewhere. But where? He scowled as his body grew cold inside his damp clothes. To warm himself and take his mind off the smell he went into the kitchen, where he fixed himself some coffee, fried eggs, bacon, sausage and toast. He found a bag, which he stuffed full of canned food. The bitch could restock the kitchen herself. That'd teach her to piss on him like she had, he thought.

An asthmatic whisper made him jerk round, dropping his food on the plate and almost making him wet himself. The thin hairs down the nape of his neck bristled as a shudder slid up his spine.

His name? Had whoever spoken whispered his name? It had been almost too faint to hear - yet close. Very close. As if whoever spoke was only inches from him.

"You left me to them."

Nobby jerked round again.

"Stinko, you bastard, where're you hidin'? Come out or I'll friggin' well break your neck, you stupid old bugger..." His words trailed off. There was no one here, he was certain. There was no one anywhere around here who could have spoken. He felt sick and stupid. And afraid. Even more afraid than when Joey Gorton had been facing him, a sawn-off shotgun aimed at his chest. His hands trembled as he picked up the gun from where he'd left it by the plate.

"They got me. When you left and legged it for all you were worth, they got me."

"Who got you, Stinko?" The tremors in his voice sickened him. He sounded pathetic. He *felt* pathetic, jabbering at

27

nothingness - at a smell that all but smothered him - and a faint, asthmatic whisper. "Who got you?"

"You friggin' well know who got me, Nobby. As soon as you'd gone they took me with them. Up on the moors. Oh God, Nobby, you shouldn't have left me. You shouldn't have let them get me, not so they could do what they did to me. It would've been better if you'd shot me."

Nobby rubbed his eyes, unable to ignore the whisperings, but even more unable to understand where they were coming from. "Where are you, Stinko? Where the friggin' Hell are you hiding?"

"Where?" The whisper faded, then came back again. *"God knows, Nobby. Hell, m'be. Or worse."* He whimpered for a moment. *"You shouldn't have left me. It weren't right, Nobby. Not when it were you as fired the shot that started it all off."*

Wiping sweat from his face, Nobby said: "I can smell and hear you, but I can't friggin' well see you."

"You'll never see me. Not till they've done to you what they did to me."

Fear catching in his voice, Nobby said: "What did they do to you, Stinko?"

There was silence for a long, long moment, and Nobby wondered if the old man, wherever he was hiding, was going to answer him or not. Finally the whisper rose once more, unnervingly close.

"They made me what I am, Nobby. Bit by bit. Enjoying what they did! Enjoying every second of what they did to me, Nobby. Every sodding second of it!"

"And now?" Sweat dripped onto his plate. "And now, Stinko? Tell me."

"I've come to tell you they're gonna get you too."

Nobby tightened his grip on the gun. His eyes jerked from side to side in the hope of catching sight of where the old man hid, though he knew deep down there was nowhere in the flat he could be hiding. "What do you mean, they're gonna get me too? They don't friggin' well know where I am."

The smell, suffocatingly strong, suddenly closed in on him

like a nauseous, impalpable gag, blocking his nose and mouth with its stench. Panic-stricken, Nobby clutched at his face. His fingers plucked at his skin in a futile effort to get rid of it.

"They know where you are, Nobby."

Clenching the gun to him, Nobby stifled a cry of terror as he picked up the keys to Marcia's car, then ran for the door. Outside in the passageway he paused, listening. For a moment he thought he had succeeded in leaving the old man's stench behind, but it was there, wafting towards him seconds later, sickeningly thick. Gritting his teeth, Nobby dashed towards the lift. When he reached it his stomach sank yet again. The indicator lights above the lift doors were flashing as the lift rose up the shaft towards him. At three in the morning Nobby knew it couldn't be anyone except the Gortons.

A flight of steps led down a gloomy, concrete stairwell next to the lift. Clenching hold of the banister rail for support he hurled himself down it, leaping two or more steps at a time in his panic to get away before the Gortons found out where he was.

Marcia's flat was on the seventh floor. By the time he reached the last flight of stairs before the hallway he was starting to become dizzy. His breath rasped between his teeth.

Steadying himself, he peered around the corner at the bottom of the stairs, relieved to see the space between the stairs, the lift and the outside doors was deserted. Hardly daring to credit his luck so far - or the sheer incompetence of the Gortons - he ran towards the doors.

For a moment the breeze that hit him outside as he burst onto the forecourt dissipated the stench that had pursued him down the stairs. But it was a false respite. Between each gust, that briefly cleared the smell from around him, it returned as strong as before.

Trying to ignore it, Nobby ran towards Marcia's Fiesta. He unlocked its door and climbed in.

Even by the time he started the car and drove off no one had appeared in an attempt to stop him, though Stinko's smell was dense inside the car. Was it stuck to his clothes? Exasperated and bewildered, Nobby steered the Fiesta onto the road, accelerating away as quickly as he could. His relief at the ease of his escape quelled some of his fears over Stinko's bizarre whisperings and the inexplicable presence of his smell. Though he could live with the old man's whispers, the smell was something else. When he got a chance he'd get rid of his clothes and buy some new ones. That and a shower would get rid of it, he thought, ignoring red lights along the way as he drove through Edgebottom. Taking the Blackburn Road, he headed towards the motorway. It was only two miles from here to the road that would take him to it. After that the Gortons could friggin' well do what they liked. They'd have a hard job tracking him to the far ends of the country, with at least a couple of hundred miles between him and the bastards, perhaps even more. He'd dump Marcia's car along the way, then take a train and lose himself completely.

If only that friggin' smell would ease up!

It made him sick, deep down in his guts. Opening the car window made no difference, as if the smell had attached itself to him. He could almost taste it. He grimaced in disgust as he wiped his mouth with the back of his hand, sweat beading his face.

"You're not gonna get away, Nobby."

He screamed, slamming his foot hard on the brakes. For a moment the car spun out of control all the way across the empty, rain-swept road, before shuddering to a halt next to the kerb, his hands clenched tight to the steering wheel as he bent dry retching over it till his throat felt raw and his chest seemed hollow.

"You friggin' bastard, Stinko," he croaked finally when the heaving of his chest had subsided. "I'll kill you." He pushed himself up from the steering wheel and glanced over his shoulder into the back of the car as if he expected to find the old man hunched there, hiding from him. But the back seat was empty.

Letting go of the steering wheel, he felt sweat drying cold on his skin as he stared at the empty seat behind him.

"Stinko?" He gulped, hardly daring to listen for the old man's reply. "Stinko, where are you? You're drivin' me mad. Show yourself to me." Urine trickled down his pants, hot against his legs. "Where are you, Stinko?"

"*Where you let them take me when you ran away.*"

"I don't know what you mean. It weren't my fault they got you. Come off it, you stupid old bugger. What do you want off of me?"

"*Help, Nobby. That's what I want off of you.*"

"What do you mean? I don't even know where you are."

"*I'll tell you, if you'll listen and do as I say.*"

"If I do, if I help you, you'll stop all of this... this stink? These whisperings?" Nobby cringed at the pathetic whine in his voice, but he couldn't help it.

"*If you help me. If you don't, I'll stay as long as you live.*" The old man whimpered, dimly, somewhere far and yet not so far away. "*I want you to get them Gortons for me. They did this to me. They put me through Hell.*"

"The Gortons?" Nobby tasted fear in his mouth, fear so vile and coppery and strong it made even the stench he'd smelt so far seem sweet by comparison. "There's no way I can get them for you, you know that."

"*You got one of them, didn't you? If you can get one, you can get more. You can get Reggie Gorton. He's the one as did it.*"

Nobby collapsed onto his seat. "Where are they?" he asked, his mind feeling numb.

"*A farm. On the hills. Just drive where I tells you.*" Stinko paused. "*You got that gun?*"

Nobby said: "It's here." He patted the pocket of his coat.

"*You'll need it.*" Stinko whimpered again as if in pain.

Nobby restarted the car. Slowly, he drove down the road, his reluctance to reach their destination fighting against his fear of what Stinko could do.

"*Take the Rossendale Road onto the moors. There's a turnoff that'll take you to the farm. I'll tell you when we've reached it.*"

The road stretched dark and wild before him, what few lamp posts there were soon petering out before he'd driven more than a mile. Only dry-stone walls and fields lay on either side, black beyond the beams of the car.

"What did they do to you?" Nobby asked, unable to stand the silence any longer.

"Did you never wonder why none of them ever got arrested for murder, even though everyone knows they've done it, again and again?"

"Course I've wondered. I've kept my mouth shut, though. Like everyone else with any sense."

"I know, Nobby. I know why. They were never done because no one ever found their bodies."

"No bodies?"

"Without a body it's hard for someone to get done for killing 'em."

Nobby stared through the windscreen as its wipers jerked back and forth, momentarily clearing it of rain.

"What happened to them?"

"You'll find out soon enough. But I'll tell you this: the Gortons are into more than robbery and violence and stuff like that."

"Such as?"

"Such as rites as'd make old Aleister Crowley himself kneel down and pray to God for help."

"Rites?" Nobby struggled with the word. "What do you mean 'rites'?"

"You stupid or something? You know what I mean. They're nutters, those Gortons. Nutters! They're into things only someone crazy would touch - because if you weren't to start with you'd be crazy soon enough later on."

Nobby stared ahead of him in silence, his brain unable to take it in. Struggling with what the old man had whispered, he felt a paralysing helplessness slowly take over as if he was still asleep and having a nightmare.

"Turn right by that knob of a hill o'er there," Stinko whispered, so close to his ear he seemed almost in it.

Nobby swung the car onto a rutted lane full of stones and

sods of grass that twisted the wheels of the car from side to side so violently the steering wheel was almost jerked from his hands and he had to grip on tight to keep control of it. He slowed to a crawl.

"Turn the lights down. Dim 'em. Or they'll see you coming."

Nobby did as he said. The surrounding moorlands seemed suddenly to stand out more clearly in the gloom. Ahead he could see a distant farmhouse, perhaps half a mile away from him yet. Its curtains glowed dim in the darkness.

"Is that it?" he asked.

"That's it." Stinko's whisper was even more hushed than before. *"That's where the bastards are."*

Nobby looked over his shoulder. Dim in the gloom at the back of the car he could make something out, a shadow within a shadow, hunched and dark. His skin prickled and he felt an almost irresistible urge to scream, to blot everything out in a hysterical shriek.

"Steady yourself, Nobby."

He clenched his fists on the steering wheel, digging his nails into the palms of his hands till they hurt.

"I'm okay," he mumbled, though he knew that he wasn't. He was far from okay.

"Pull over. If you go much further they'll hear the car."

The engine died, leaving a silence marred only by the winds still blowing across the moors. Nobby reached for the gun in his pocket. He felt an overwhelming need for its reassurance suddenly, though he knew there were only three bullets left. Three bullets against how many Gortons? he wondered.

"Come on. Stir your stumps," Stinko whispered. *"Get a move on. It won't come to you."*

Nobby fastened his coat against the gusts of wind that buffeted him as he climbed out of the car. He bowed his head against the wind as he picked his way down the lane, his feet stumbling in potholes in its muddy surface.

Soon chilled by the dampness of his clothes, Nobby shivered as he hunched his shoulders. The only improvement was that

Stinko's smell was barely noticeable in the open air as the wind lashed hard into his face, snatching the breath from his mouth - and snatching Stinko's smell away with it.

It took more than quarter of an hour to trudge the rest of the way to the farmhouse. A five-bar gate hung loose at the entrance. Sliding past, Nobby noticed a car parked across the otherwise empty farmyard. He recognized it as the limousine he saw the previous day in the quarry when they met the Gortons.

Ignoring the panic in his stomach, Nobby stole towards the building. For a moment he sheltered in the lee of its walls, before moving on and creeping towards the edge of the nearest window.

Nobby licked his rain-wetted lips, narrowing his eyes as he peeped through a gap in the curtains. Beams of light, directed from spot lamps positioned about the room inside, converged on the naked body of what had once been a man, hung from ropes fastened to hooks in the ceiling. For a moment the oddity of the body's stance puzzled Nobby. For some reason it looked wrong. Only after he had been staring at it for a few minutes did he realise why. The man's legs had been broken at the knees. Ropes fastened to the blood-covered ankles had pulled the lower part of the man's legs forwards. The same had been done to his arms, beaten into a bloody pulp at their joints and bent backwards.

Nobby could not see the man's face. His head was slumped on his chest. Probably dead, Nobby thought, as he grimaced at the ugly wounds covering what was left of his skin, whole sections of which had been flayed from his chest and stomach to hang like a tattered skirt about his waist. Blood had dried in crusts about the exposed sinews, fat, arteries and veins.

Even as he peered with horrified fascination at the corpse's head, Nobby was certain he knew who it was. He could not fail to recognise the grey hair hanging from it, glistening with sweat. He didn't need to be able to smell him to know it was Stinko. Nobby turned away, disgust and nausea - *and fear* - filling him. He leaned against the house, too weak to move. Stinko had spoken to him only minutes ago. Again and again he'd heard his

34

whisper. And smelt his stench. Yet the man was hanging only yards away from him, mutilated and dead, his arms and legs broken and bent out of shape. Nobby shook his head blindly, his eyes shut tight. It couldn't be. It couldn't.

Someone moved inside the house. He heard heavy footsteps creak across the bare floorboards, audible even through the window. Nobby recognised Reggie Gorton at once. He was stood, staring at Stinko's body, a can of lager in one hand and a half-eaten pie in the other.

What the friggin' Hell was the bastard up to? Nobby wondered in disgust, tasting bile in his throat as, for the first time, he started to feel pity for what had happened to Stinko. What kind of tortures had the bastards put the old man through before he croaked? Nobby felt sick in his stomach as he thought about it.

"*You see what I mean?*" The old man's stench crept near him again.

Nobby shivered. "I see."

"*And now?*"

"Now what? Shoot him?" Nobby felt weak with fear. Fear at what he couldn't understand. Fear at the pain, the tortures, the hideous cruelties the Gortons were capable of inflicting on their victims. Fear of what would happen to him if they caught him now - or if he did what Stinko wanted him to do and failed.

"*Shoot him, Nobby. If you don't, they'll get you. Sooner or later, they'll get you too.*"

Nobby shook his head, unable to act - unable to do anything.

"*Shoot him, Nobby. You've got to.*"

"I can't." Sweat covered him. It dripped from his face, running thick with salt into his mouth. "I can't."

Stinko whimpered with frustration - and pain, as if he still felt the tortures he'd been inflicted with in the farmhouse. Nobby turned to the sound. Was there something there, waiting in the shadows? The impression was vague, so intangibly faint he couldn't be sure.

"Why?" Nobby asked. "Why have you come to me?"

Stinko must have moved closer, because his smell became suddenly stronger than before.

"Look, Nobby - look and see!"

Nobby turned and stared through the window again.

Reggie Gorton was not alone in the room. Three other men stood there. One of them lounged nonchalantly against the open door into the inner hallway. They were talking, but Nobby could barely make out more than a murmur. For the first time, though, he noticed the signs and symbols daubed across the bare white walls - daubed in what might have been blood. They looked evil, with jagged curves and lines, more like implements of torture than letters.

Nobby felt as if he should cross himself, but too many years had passed since the religious teachings Father Donnelly at St. Mary's had tried to drum into him when he was a boy. Instead Nobby stared into the room with a sense of numbness, unaware at first that Stinko's smell had gone. No trace of it lingered now. When he realised this, Nobby sniffed suspiciously. Stinko had gone, he was sure. But why had he deserted him now?

Staring through the window, Nobby saw that Gorton had finished his pie and was stood in front of Stinko's body, his head tilted back as he swigged the last of his lager. Emptying it, he crushed the can and tossed it to one side. He raised his hands towards Stinko. His thick fingers touched the old man's chest, its raw flesh glistening with blood that had still to dry completely. Tacky, it stuck to the gangster's fingers as he drew them from it and put them to his mouth, licking them clean. Vomit threatened to rise inside Nobby's throat, and he had to force the bile back as he gritted his teeth in disgust.

Reggie Gorton produced a knife from inside his jacket. It was curiously curved. For stripping skin? Nobby wondered. The gangster stroked it down the dead man's shoulder, digging deep into his flesh, before he reached out with his other hand. He pushed his fingers beneath the dead man's rib cage, nudging them upwards towards where the heart had to be.

Nobby felt blood drain from his face.

The body moved, twisting sideways.

Reggie Gorton pushed harder.

And Stinko shrieked.

Even Nobby, outside in the wind and rain, could hear the old man's scream, as Stinko threw back his head and stared at Gorton, so much agony and despair transfixed on his ravaged, mutilated face.

But he was dead. Nobby knew it. He had to be dead. There was no way the old man could still be alive, not with so much skin peeled from him?

Besides, Nobby realised, he had heard and spoken with his ghost. He'd smelt it.

Stinko was dead. He couldn't be alive. Not now.

Yet he moved. And cried. And bled as Gorton worked on his body, cutting and slicing, peeling and plunging and removing objects from deep inside him.

Nobby felt for the gun. He pulled it from his pocket and checked that it still had three shells left in its chambers.

When he looked back again Reggie Gorton had succeeded in flaying most of Stinko's shoulder. The bared flesh glistened with bright red blood. Fresh blood.

"You friggin', fuckin' bastard," Nobby muttered to himself as he raised the gun and aimed with both hands, gripping it tight. "You friggin', lousy, stinkin' bastard." He pulled on the trigger. There was a loud, almost deafening crack. Flames shot from the barrel. Glass shattered, blowing inwards as Nobby felt the heavy jolt of the gun kick in his hands, his eyes transfixed on Gorton's head. Or what remained of it as the bullet, distorted by the glass it had smashed its way through, burst bones and brain from its path before erupting in a plume of spray from the other side.

Gorton stiffened, as if hit by a massive bolt of electricity, his left leg twitching as he fell to the floor with a resounding crash.

The other men stared for an instant at the shattered window, and Nobby was able to fire once more before they turned and fled the room. Using the gun, Nobby smashed the rest of the windowpane, before hauling himself inside. Ignoring the two bodies, he ran towards the door, but the hallway was already deserted. Outside he could hear a car starting up. Breathless, he rushed to the window in time to catch sight of the car in the farmyard setting off. He fired at it, though whether he hit anything he wasn't sure. The car surged forwards, smashing through the five-bar gate, before heading at breakneck speed down the lane.

"Fuckin' idiots," Nobby muttered. Seconds later there was a squeal of brakes. The thunderous explosion that came instants later was accompanied by a massive ball of flames that highlighted the fields in its glare.

He'd have to friggin' well walk away now, Nobby thought as he watched the smoke and flames where the gangsters' car had smashed into the Fiesta he'd left down the lane.

"You did well."

Nobby shuddered. His flesh ran cold as he turned to face what remained of Stinko hung from the ropes.

"What were those friggin' bastards into?" Nobby asked, his voice little more than a hushed whisper as he stared at the obscure markings on the walls.

Stinko coughed what may have been a laugh. It was the best his ravaged, ruined body could do. *"Their own mad passions,"* the old man said. *"Their own mad demons."*

"I thought you were dead." Nobby strode towards him, though the sight of what was left of the old man made him sick to his stomach.

The old man moved his head a little. It wobbled on the flayed stalk of his neck.

"I thought it were your ghost that came to me," Nobby said.

"How d'you know it weren't? How d'you know I'm not dead?"

Nobby froze.

"Fools like the Gortons use people like Stinko to conjure and trap us in their tortured flesh. It wasn't the old man they were torturing here when you looked in." The figure straightened. Its limbs moved on their broken joints as if they were meant to be that way. *"They knew all about me. They used me to help them."* It sniggered wetly.

Nobby grunted as he started to back away from him. Stinko's face was changing. It was changing too much.

It was changing too fast.

"*They knew how to make me do what they wanted me to do. They knew how to keep me trapped.*"

The thing that was Stinko hauled itself free of the ropes holding it.

"*You know nothing about me, nothing at all...*" It paused for a moment, a form of humour on its bloody face as it bent beside the body of Reggie Gorton, held one of his hands, then tugged at a finger, tearing it free like a child plucking fruit. It glanced at the finger, then slid it appreciatively into its mouth. "*No, Nobby, you know nothing about me... yet.*"

LOCK-IN

"Nobody expects anything really dramatic to happen at Christmas."

"There was Ceausescu. He got toppled at Christmas. That was pretty dramatic."

"And they shot him. Which was even more dramatic."

"Along with his wife!"

"Then we had the Tsunami on Boxing Day."

"I know that, I know. But - and it's a big <u>but</u> – it's still true that no one expects anything to happen at Christmas. When it does, it takes us by surprise."

"But you could say that about any day of the year. You could say no one expects anything really dramatic to happen on the twenty-fifth of July. Now there's a boring date for you."

"And if you said this to the vicar he'd soon tell you that the most dramatic event in the history of mankind happened at Christmas."

"Oh, put a sock in it! You'll have us singing carols next. For God's sake…"

"Anyway, Bob, what exactly are you getting at? Why does it matter whether, rightly or wrongly – depending on your point of view – you think no one expects anything really dramatic to happen at Christmas? Apart for the usual domestic break-ups and rows and everything else you might expect when most of the population over indulges in alcohol."

"Never mind all that. Whose round is it next? I'm drinking without." Arthur Renshaw banged his empty beer glass on the table between them, emphasising his point. The four old men, the Grudgers they called themselves (after the district of town they were all born in, Grudge End), burst out laughing, while Bob Beesley fished in his wallet for a ten-pound note.

"Barman," he called out. "Another four of your best, please!"

They were a distinctive group, even in the Potter's Wheel, one of the few unrefurbished, unremodernised pubs in the district. Its dark wallpaper first saw the light of day – such as ever penetrated this far – over thirty years ago, much about the same time the paint dried on its woodwork. There was a luxurious atmosphere of dilapidation about the place, with its damp beer mats that often stuck tenaciously to the scarred wooden tables and the old fashioned, barrel-shaped glasses.

Bob Beesley heaved himself up off his stool and waddled to the bar, where he picked up their next round of drinks and passed them, one by one, to eager hands held stretched from the nearby alcove that was literally their own reserve spot in the pub. "And a bag of pork scratchings," Bob added. "I'm feelin' a bit peckish."

By the time he'd sat down again, panting from the effort, the others had taken at least two or three gulps of their beers and were busily arguing once more. Bob pushed his thick, horn-rimmed spectacles back up the broad bridge of his nose and glanced at the darkening sky outside the nearest window as he nimbly unfastened his pork scratchings. It looked as if there was a storm brewing, which probably meant he'd have to hurry home later to avoid getting soaked; he'd left his raincoat hung behind his front door, along with his brolly. Typical the weather should change like this, he thought. Just his luck.

"Anyway," Tom Atkins said to him; his sallow cheeks had gained a faint, almost healthy flush from the two pints he'd drunk, "what's all this about Christmas? It's not November till tomorrow. It's only friggin' Halloween tonight. It's bad enough all the shops start putting up their blasted decorations as soon as we've seen the back of Bonfire Night, without you going on about it."

"You old humbug," Arthur scolded him. "You get more miserable by the year."

"So would you if you'd thirteen grandchilder to buy presents for – and none of 'em cheap."

"As if you didn't really love it," Bob told him. "I've seen

42

you, hiking off to Eddison's Toy Shop on Market Street. You're like a child yourself when you get in there. And I'll bet you make sure you help some of those grandchilder of yours to play with their toys!"

The others laughed, including Tom, who had to admit that he did, sometimes, have to help them out. "But only when they're not sure how to play with them properly," he added. "Some of these modern toys are very complicated to use, you know."

Paddy Morgan, his brick-red cheeks like very old slabs of beef, shook his head sadly. "You never grew up, Tom. I've always said it."

"Some of us grow up too fast," Tom told him. "I envy my grandchilder. They've some wonderful toys these days. Far better than we'd to make do with when we were kiddies."

There was a rumbled chorus of agreements to this. Then Tom said: "I'd better get in another round. I see Arthur's about to be drinking without again."

"Drinks too fast. Always has. Like a bottomless drain," Bob grumbled good-naturedly. He glanced at the clock, hidden above the bar amidst a line of almost empty optics. Nine thirty and he felt tired already. Getting old, he thought. Getting far too old. Not like the old days when the four of them would paint the town red. A long, long time ago now, he added to himself, sadly.

Apart from the four of them there were only a few regulars in the pub tonight. Midweek, though, it was always quiet. Which suited the Grudgers. None of them cared for the weekends, when the Potter's Wheel was crammed with youngsters, and Sam Sowerby, the landlord, switched on the normally silent juke box.

"What's going on out there?"

On his way to the bar, Tom glanced at the speaker, a terse old farmer who drove down to the pub at night in his battered Land Rover for a pint or two by himself before going home to bed.

"What is it, Jim?" Tom asked as he leant against the bar and nodded to the landlord for another four pints..

"Outside. Looks like some sort of commotion. Might be some damned idiots out celebrating Halloween." Jim Bartlet slammed down his beer and sidled over to the frosted glass door. Frowning, he placed a hand on the door knob to pull it open.

As he watched him, Tom felt a faint premonition that something was wrong, something worse than just a commotion outside. And for an instant he had an urge to tell Jim to ignore it, to let go of the door and go back to the bar. But it was an urge he ignored. Not only would Jim think he was being absurd, but he would take no notice of him. In fact, he'd be even more likely to go ahead with whatever he was going to do if he said anything to him. And quite rightly so. If someone told Tom something as ridiculous as that he'd ignore them as well. Tom shuddered, though, as the irascible old farmer pulled the door open and stepped outside. There was a brief hint of fog and a noise like someone snapping twigs. Less than a minute later the door burst open and Jim Bartlet fell back into the pub, blood streaming from his face. He made a half turn, as if to steady himself against the bar, then slithered to the ground. Tom reached for him, but his reflexes were slow these days and he missed. Sam Sowerby, though, for all his own weight, was round the public side of the bar within seconds and knelt beside the farmer, cradling his head. Jim's face was unrecognisable. A red, raw ruin of sinews and veins and stripped, naked meat. It was as if the skin had been sliced from his face, cut away from deep into the flesh and muscles and down into the bone. On instinct Tom went to the heavy, wooden outer door, hurriedly closed it with a solid thud, then snapped the locks shut, top and bottom, though it seemed a feeble enough defence against whatever had attacked Jim Bartlet.

The rest of the Grudgers had scrambled to their feet, even Bill, though he trailed behind the others as they gathered about the body on the floor.

"I'll phone for the police," Arthur said. He hurried to the

phone behind the bar. A moment later he looked at the others, a crestfallen expression on his long, thin, lugubrious face. "It's dead," he told them.

Bob frowned at him. "What d'you mean *dead*?"

"It's dead," Arthur repeated. "The phone's dead."

Sam laid the farmer's mutilated head back on the floor. "Let me try," he told him. He hurried behind the bar and stabbed energetically at the buttons on the phone, as if force alone could make it work. In the end he slammed it back on its cradle. He looked over at the locked outer door. The others, watching him, looked over too.

"I ain't going out there. Not till there's at least a vanful of police outside. Preferably a SWAT team," Bob muttered.

"I don't think there's much chance of a SWAT team in Edgebottom," Tom told him. "Not for hours anyway. They'd have to send to Manchester for one - and that's more than fifteen mile frae here."

Paddy nodded at the dead body of Jim Bartlet. "What the 'ell did that to him? We can't just stand here while there's someone out there who killed poor Jim like that. It's horrible. Horrible. We've got to contact the police. Somehow."

"Barring smoke signals – which no one would see at this time of night anyway – what would you suggest, Paddy?" Sam asked, shaken; he looked down at his bloodstained hands, then went to the sink behind the bar to wash them clean. "What would you suggest?" he muttered to himself as he vigorously tried to wipe them dry on a wet bar towel.

"There's a lunatic out there," Bob said. "A lunatic with a butcher's cleaver. What else could have done that to Jim Bartlet's face?"

They all, reluctantly, looked down at the farmer's head, laid in a spreading pool of blood. The only other customer left in the pub beside the Grudgers was Harold Sillitoe, a retired schoolmaster with literary pretensions. But he seemed speechless, sat on his barstool with his eyes closed against the horror only three yards from him, his single malt whisky untouched on the bar in front of him.

"What did he hear that made him go outside?" Paddy wondered out loud.

"Whatever it was I couldn't hear it." Tom shook his head. "But I did feel something was wrong. I almost said that to him. That he'd be better off ignoring whatever he'd heard and stay here. I don't even know why I felt that. Though I wish I'd said something now."

"And do you think Jim would've listened?" Bob asked. "He'ld've told you to stop being soft. And gone out."

"At least I would've tried. I feel guilty somehow."

"Bollocks! Only the bastard as did that to him is guilty of anything. How were you to know someone would chop off his friggin' face?" Bob reached for his pint off the table behind them and took a long swallow.

"We've still got to do something," Paddy insisted. "We can't just stay here while whoever attacked him is still out there, roaming about."

The landlord shook his head. "And what would you suggest? I've tried the phone. And that's dead. What else is there?"

"You've got a mobile, haven't you?" Paddy asked.

Sam swore, then hurried to the stairs. He came back again only a minute later, mobile in one hand. "No signal. No bloody signal."

A tense silence settled on the men. Then Bob asked if Sam had the remote for the TV. There was an old, eighteen-inch set in the games room, usually used by some of the locals to watch horse racing on Saturday afternoons, though none of the Grudgers had ever watched it.

Sam disappeared behind the bar, then came out with the remote and went into the games room, with its pool table and darts board. They heard him cursing to himself. The old men exchanged worried looks, then Sam strode slowly back into the lounge, his broad face even paler than usual.

"You aren't going to believe this," he said to them.

46

"But you can't get any channels," Bob answered. "The TV's dead as well."

"No reception on any of its channels." Sam flung the remote onto the bar. "It's as if we're cut off from everything."

"But how?" Bob asked.

"And why?" Tom put in with a shudder. "Why?"

Bob wandered slowly to the window and peered outside, the others watching him intently. He moved his head cautiously from side to side, but the darkness looked impenetrable. He couldn't even see any street lights down the road. Not far away should have been the illuminated clock tower on St Paul's Junior School. He couldn't see that either. Nor the traffic lights at the end of the block. Nor any traffic. No traffic at all. As if the world outside had ceased to exist.

Shuddering, Bob backed away from the window. He looked at the others, unsure what to say.

"This is freakin' surreal," Sillitoe suddenly said, reaching for his whisky. "Freakin', freakin' surreal."

"Calm down, Harold," the landlord told him. "No need to panic."

The others eyed him in disbelief.

"If this isn't cause enough to panic, what is?" Bob asked.

The rest added their agreement.

"I'm just about ready to panic myself," Tom said. "And that's without even knowing what 'freaking surreal' even means."

Perhaps in an effort to show some kind of moral control, Sam slowly walked towards the front door.

"Are you sure what you're doing?" Tom asked.

"We can't just stay here, can we?" Sam said, uncertainly.

"But if you go out, the same might happen to you as happened to Jim Bartlet. I wouldn't risk it."

"Nor me," added Bob.

Sam looked round at them, seeing the concern in their faces. The fear.

"We can't just wait around for something to happen," Sam

told them, insistently.

With less resolution than he allowed himself to show, Sam took a firm hold of the upper lock of the front door, then clicked it open. Bending his knees, he reached for the lower lock and clicked that open too. Licking his lips, Sam paused for a moment to rebuild his determination, before reaching for the door handle, his palm damp with sweat as he tried to grip it as firmly as he could.

The door opened with ease. Outside all was black, the solid, impenetrable black of absolute nothingness. No street lights, no traffic, no hint of the stars or the moon or the pavement or the rest of the town or anything of the outside world at all. Just an endless, eternal black, like everlasting night, that went on and on till his eyes ached from the strain of staring into it.

Even so, Sam stood at the pub doorway for a long, long moment. He wanted to reach out into the darkness, but something warned him not to do it, that not only would it be wrong but dangerous. Perhaps Jim Bartlet had felt the same urge and leant out to peer into the darkness too, and in doing so lost his face. Sam shuddered, unable to cope with the bizarre ideas that rushed in at him about what he was looking at, then he stepped back into the warmth and light and shabby cosiness of the pub; he slammed the front door shut behind him and returned to the lounge.

"What did you see?" Bob asked, a tremor in his voice.

"Come on," Tom added. "Say something. You're worrying me."

Sam stepped behind the bar and poured himself a stiff whisky from the optics. He drank it in one gulp, then poured himself another. He drank this too in one gulp.

"Sam!" Bob rapped on the bar to catch his attention. "What the hell did you see?"

"See?" Sam shut his eyes for a moment, his plump face blank. "I wish there had been something to see. But I couldn't see nothing more than you could see through the window. There's nothing. Nothing out there. Nothing at all."

48

"Stop talking nonsense," Paddy snapped at him. "What d'you mean, nothing? D'you mean you couldn't see anything because we've had a power cut?"

"A power cut that's affected everywhere apart from the Potter's Wheel?" Sam laughed humourlessly. "You're a genius, Paddy. How come I couldn't think of that!"

"Then what?" Bob asked. Feeling queasy with fear, he sat down on one of the old bar stools and leant against the bar. He felt in need of his pint of beer again.

"There's no 'what' about it. Not so far as I can see - so far as I can reckon," Sam said, almost to himself. "I looked out of the door and there was nothing there. Just a deep black void that went on and on forever."

"Steady, Sam," Tom told him.

"Steady? You should take a look out there yourself," Sam said. "But be careful, 'cause I reckon it's a blackness you shouldn't even try to touch. Not unless you want to end up like Jim."

"I thought some madman did that to him. Hacked him with a knife or an axe," Paddy said, as they looked down at the farmer's body by the bar.

Sam shook his head. "I don't think so. There's nothing human, mad or otherwise, out there, Paddy. Whatever did that to him wasn't human. More likely it was just the blackness that did it. How, I don't know."

The six men sat round the bar for some minutes in silence as each of them tried to digest what had happened.

Suddenly, his face white with fear, Harold Sillitoe knocked over his whisky and rushed for the door. "I don't care what rubbish any of you say, I'm not staying here," he shouted at them. "I'm not staying here to be trapped."

Sam tried to grab his arm, but the schoolteacher was too fast. The next moment he reached the door, snapped its locks and flung it open. Arthur Renshaw was the nearest to him; he tried to pull him back, but Sillitoe was too determined to get out of the pub, and slipped past his fingers. The moment he reached beyond the doorway into the darkness, though, he screamed. At that instant Arthur managed to grasp hold of the collar of his coat, then grunted with the effort as he tugged him back. Together they fell into the lounge, tumbling across the floor, as Sillitoe writhed in abject agony, the stumps of his arms jetting blood over the two of them. Tom moved in and pulled Arthur free, then stood back as the schoolteacher's body spasmed, then stilled, and the blood ceased pumping from the severed ends of his arms.

A look of horror on his face, Arthur said: "What the hell did that to him?"

"I told you," Sam answered. "The darkness. He touched it. He put his arms into it. And, somehow, in some way, it destroyed them."

"Like acid?"

"Or worse."

"Much worse," Bob added sombrely. "I saw what acid can do when I worked at Watson's Chemical Works in Thrushington and that's nothing like as bad as this, believe me. Nor anything like so fast." He shuddered and sat down again on his stool. Then reached for his beer.

Meanwhile Sam knelt beside Sillitoe. "He's dead," he told them, though they knew this by now. The schoolteacher's body had jerked only once and become so still there was no room for doubt in any of them that he had died – that and the stemming of the outpouring of blood from what was left of his arms.

Sam nodded to Arthur, and the two of them dragged Sillitoe's body away to one wall. They then dragged Jim Bartlet's next to it, away from the bar.

"Place is beginning to look like a friggin' morgue," Tom muttered.

"Aye, and it's us who are creatin' it," Bob added.

Sam went behind the bar, filled five glasses of whisky, then passed them out to the four Grudgers, before sitting down himself and taking a deep gulp of his drink. "I hope that's the last attempt any of us make to get out through that door."

With an exchange of glances the four men nodded their heads as they raised the whiskies to their lips.

"What are we going to do?" Bob asked. "We can't just sit here, pleasant though it is, forever."

"Well, I'm just glad my wife decided to leave me last month," Sam said. "Otherwise the nagging bitch'd be going at us relentlessly by now."

"What d'you reckon it is?" Paddy asked.

Sam shrugged. "I've no more idea than any of you. I doubt our schoolteacher friend, for all his learning and degrees and suchlike, had any more himself. Which is, perhaps, why he panicked."

As the hours passed the five men slowly relapsed into silence. It was only when it passed eleven o'clock, when he would normally lock the front door and call last orders, that Sam remembered his lodger. Ever since his wife left him, he had supplemented his dwindling income in the pub by letting out one of the spare bedrooms upstairs. An odd old bugger, his current lodger called himself Albert Durer, though Sam was sure this wasn't his real name somehow. Still, the money was welcome each week – and he paid it on time every Friday.

"Have any of you seen Albert?" Sam asked, though none of the men remembered catching sight of the lodger all evening.

"Perhaps he couldn't get in 'cause of that stuff," Paddy suggested, with a vague gesture at the door.

"I'll go take a look in his room," Sam said.

It was less than a minute later that he shouted down to the rest of them to "come up here! For Christ's sake, take a look at this!"

As the four men gathered about the open doorway upstairs, panting for breath, Sam stood at the far end of the room in front of the curtained window. Between them the threadbare carpet had been rolled back to uncover the floorboards. On these there was a large, painted circle in white and a five-pointed star. All around the edges were peculiar symbols and the burnt-out stubs of candles, their melted wax lying in off-white ridges on the floorboards. In the centre of the star was what horrified them all the most: it was a nailed-down body of a rat, its ribs and stomach sliced open.

"The dirty bastard," Bob muttered, wiping sweat from his forehead. "The dirty, *dirty* bastard!"

"Filthy pervert, more like," Tom put in. "Who'd do a thing like that?"

"Albert Durer, that's who," Sam said. "And here's me, cookin' his breakfast for him every morning, and the bastard does that in my own home."

"What is it?" Paddy asked. "Satanism?"

"I don't know," Sam said. "It's something horrible, I know that. Whether it's Satanism or not, I haven't a clue. Ask me something I know something about and I'll answer you. This…this is just friggin' disgustin', whatever you call it."

"There's some kind of old book over there on the dresser," Tom said, pointing.

They followed his finger, and Sam stepped over to the dresser, gingerly keeping his feet outside the painted circle. He touched the open book, its pages crackling beneath his fingers like very old parchment. He stared at it hard for several moments, his brows puckering with concentration.

"Can't make out a blessed thing that's written in it," he told them eventually. "It's all in some kind of foreign language."

"Like French?" Paddy asked, to whom foreign meant Calais, which was the furthest he'd ever travelled.

"Or Latin?" Bob asked, who'd done four years of it at Grammar School a long time ago and could just about remember Amo, Amas, Amat.

"Take a look," Sam told him, but when Bob sidled over to peer at the book, he shook his head. "I don't think it is Latin," he said finally. "Or if it is, it's in some kind of code."

The men shook their heads in consternation.

"D'you think this has anything to do with what's happened tonight?" Tom asked.

Sam stared at him. "That blackness?" he asked.

"I know it sounds mad," Tom went on. "But before what happened to Jim and Harold that would have sounded mad too. And it is Halloween. When better to do something queer like this?"

"But why?" Bob asked. "And how?"

Tom shrugged. "You'd have to ask Sam's absent lodger that, if we ever get chance to meet him again."

"I'd like just one chance to meet that bastard again," Sam muttered as he gazed at the mutilated remains of the rat nailed to the floorboards. "He'd not forget it if we did."

While they were upstairs, they checked the rest of the bedrooms and Sam's living room, but the sheer solid blackness outside never changed. By the early hours of the morning they had all gone to sleep in the two other bedrooms besides Durer's, though none of them felt secure enough to undress. Whatever was happening to them, they were sure there were more surprises in store. And none of them, probably, good.

Sam was the first up. By half eight he had prepared breakfast for them all of fried eggs and bacon.

"There's plenty of food in the freezer, but I can't promise many more days of bacon and egg," he told them as they sat about the table in the kitchen.

"Do you think we'll be stuck here that long?" Tom asked, his sallow complexion now grey, with dark shadows under his eyes.

"Who knows?" Sam said. "We're still stuck now, aren't we? Which makes it nearly twelve hours already. Who knows how much longer this'll go on?"

"Much longer and I think I'll go stir crazy," Tom muttered. "We might've joked sometimes about how grand it'd be to get locked inside a pub, but the reality's not quite the same."

"The lock-in from Hell," Bob said. Like Tom, his plump face showed signs of strain.

"I never thought the Potter's Wheel Paradise, but I never reckoned to compare it to Hell," Sam said with an attempt at levity, trying to put out of his mind what they saw in Albert Durer's bedroom.

Levity, though, had come into short supply by mid-afternoon and the view through the windows was still pitch black. There was a creeping atmosphere of fear in the pub. And claustrophobia.

There were strange anomalies. Though they could neither send nor receive telephone calls, and the TV and radio were dead, there were still supplies of electricity and water. Arthur Renshaw said it was a pity the water pipes weren't big enough to crawl along, otherwise they might have been able to get out that way, till Bob pointed out that, however big the pipes might be, they would drown in them anyway because of the water – and still get nowhere. Sam organised for the two bodies in the lounge to be wrapped and taped inside bin bags, then he and Tom dragged them into the cellar, where it was cold enough to keep them preserved – and where, more importantly, they weren't in constant view.

By evening there was real fear.

"We should have heard something from someone by now," Tom insisted. "Surely somebody knows we're stuck here, that something's wrong."

Sam shrugged. "Who knows what it's like on the outside? Perhaps it's as dangerous to get into the Potter's Wheel as it is to get out."

They drank slowly and steadily that night. Talk petered out long before ten; after that they sat around the bar in desultory groups, each consumed by their own gloomy thoughts for the future. Before they knew it, it was midnight, they all felt slightly drunk, and went to bed grumbling about the bloody absurdity of it all.

Five days passed and the situation hardly changed, though the bacon and eggs for breakfast had long since run out and Sam was beginning to look increasingly more worried whenever he went to the freezer. His initial optimism about what it held hadn't taken into account that it would have to cater for five grown men, with no additional food coming in from any other source. Now it was beginning to empty with ominous speed.

Two days later the freezer was down to an already opened bag of peas, three fish fingers, some ice cream in a battered tub and a very old packet of boil-in-the-bag spinach.

Within the next few days they were all beginning to feel hungry and beginning to realise that they were facing the grim prospect of starvation. If being imprisoned within the pub had been enough to make them feel afraid to start with, their food running out increased this till there was hardly a moment when they weren't aware of it. It dominated their thoughts. But there was nothing they could do about it. They had long since searched the pub for every possible scrap of food, from half eaten packets of biscuits to the snacks hung on cards behind the bar. Even dusty jars of out of date cherries for cocktails that had never been popular in the Potter's Wheel had all been consumed. Their ill-assorted diet led them to feeling queasy as well as hungry, depressing their spirits even more and making all of them irritable.

By the end of the second week tempers, as well as hunger, were at breaking point...

"This is bloody ridiculous," Bob said eventually as the five of them sat around a table in the lounge. With empty stomachs, they had stopped drinking alcohol till later at night; and each of them now held a bottle of fruit juice from behind the bar. "We've got to do something. If we don't, we're going to starve to death within the next couple of weeks, unless we turn to cannibalism."

"And with only five of us that wouldn't last long," Sam put in with a rueful smile, though his attempt at humour met with little response from the drawn faces of the four old men, who stared at him in silence

"We've got to try something," Tom said. "Even if it means risking what happened to the others. If we don't..."

"If we don't, we're doomed," Bob said flatly.

Sam went behind the bar and poured them five beers. "If we're to plan getting out of here we need something stronger than orange juice," he told them.

Their first plans, though, were vague impracticalities that were soon dissected and tossed to one side. It was Tom who came up with the first and only practical suggestion.

"Have you ever wondered why we've still got water and electricity?" he asked.

"Good job we have them," Arthur said. "We'd have been well buggered if we hadn't."

"I agree with you there. But *why* have we still got them," Tom went on insistently. "That's the important thing. That's what I've been wondering. After all, we've no TV or radio signals."

They sat there watching him, waiting.

"And?" Bob asked. "What answer have you come up with? Or is this going to be twenty friggin' questions?"

"Two things," Tom said, and, despite the hunger that was aching in his stomach, he managed a smile of monumental smugness. "Electrical cable and lead pipes – or whatever they make water pipes from these days."

"It ain't lead, I know that," Sam said. "But I get your point. Electricity and water get through because they're protected in some kind of casing."

"And?" Bob asked. "Am I being a bit thick, but how does that help us. We can't get out of here through either of them, can we?"

"But we might be able to make some kind of casing through the darkness," Tom said. "Something that'll protect us inside. It's just a matter of finding something that'll stretch out into the darkness that we would be safe inside."

"It's more than just worth a try," Sam said. "Better than sitting here, starving to death."

Putting aside their beers, they set out foraging about the pub for materials they could use to construct a tunnel.

"I hope that darkness doesn't stretch too far," Tom confided in Sam, but the landlord shrugged. "We've got to try, Tom. It's the best idea so far, and if we don't make a stab at it we're doomed anyway."

It was in the beer cellar they came up with the solution. At one time, during the late eighties, a previous landlord had made an attempt at building up the catering side of the pub, and with that purpose in mind had started work on a proper professional kitchen. Things had gone well, till he was told he would have to construct a ventilation system. Spiralling costs, at each new demand from the local council, had resulted in him eventually abandoning the project. In the cellar, though, were the aluminium panels for an unconstructed ventilation system, ready to be connected together to form a two-foot square metal shaft.

"If we could connect these together we could lead them from the front door out into the darkness. Hopefully they'll make a shaft long enough to let us crawl out of here," Sam said, as they relayed the open-ended boxes up the cellar steps to the bar.

Opening the front door was a ticklish operation as no one wanted to risk suffering any of the mutilations that struck those who had already tried to get out that way. The deep, almost cosmic darkness that confronted them, with its cold, black depths, had become no less awesome – or frightening. Gingerly, they pushed the ventilation shaft, a twelve-foot length of aluminium squares, inch by inch out across the doorstep into what should have been the street. Their first attempt, though, was a dismal failure. As they shone a torch into it, they could see that the inexplicable darkness had entered it from the far end, filling it till it was in line with the darkness at the doorstep.

"We'll need to seal the far end off," Sam said as they pulled the shaft back into the pub. "Perhaps that'll keep it out."

They found some sheets of aluminium in the cellar which fitted on the end of the shaft. With a soldering iron, it did not take long before they had it in place.

"Make sure you seal in every gap, otherwise the darkness might seep through," Tom suggested while Sam worked on it. "But not too strongly. It has to break off."

This time, as they slowly, carefully pushed the delicate shaft into the darkness, the inside remained clear. Even when most of it stretched out from the pub, its outside swallowed by the darkness around it, as if it no longer existed, its interior remained bright, unsullied by even the slightest hint of darkness.

The five men exchanged cheers of jubilation. They sat back and admired their work for a moment.

"Do you think the far end's reached the other side of the darkness?" Arthur asked, dampening their spirits. None of them knew how far the darkness reached. For all they knew it might have stretched only inches from the pub – or gone on for eternity. There was no way they could tell from staring into it. It was black and impenetrable to their gaze.

"There's only one way to tell," Sam said. "One of us is going to have to creep along that shaft and batter the end off with a hammer. Then, either the darkness will flood in, or there'll be the real world again."

"You make it sound so simple," Bob said. "But you do realise, don't you, that if the shaft doesn't reach safety and the darkness does come flooding in, whoever's in there will be swallowed by it?"

"And be dissolved like poor old Jim Bartlett's face or Harold Sillitoe's arms," Tom said, unable to hide the horror in his voice as he said it.

"Thanks, Tom," Sam told him. "I was trying to forget that alternative."

"Well, one of us will have to try it, whatever the risks. Otherwise we've just wasted our time." Bob wiped his hands on his knees. He looked down at his stomach, which still loomed large despite their enforced diet. "Though I don't suppose I'll be able to volunteer. I might manage to squeeze down that shaft, but I don't think I'd be able to move my arms enough to use a hammer to force the end off."

"I think we'll need someone somewhat slimmer, I agree." Sam looked at the others, conscious that, even though he was youngest here, he was not much slimmer than Bob, and would have a problem in the tunnel too. "Well?" he asked. "Who is it going to be?"

There was a long moment of silence. The others knew the dangers involved, that whoever crawled along the shaft and knocked off the end would be risking his life.

"One of us'll have to do it," Arthur said. "Perhaps we should toss for it or pick a short straw or something like that."

The only ones slim enough to make it, Paddy, Arthur and Tom, exchanged glances.

Sam nipped behind the bar. He returned a minute later with a pack of playing cards.

"Lowest card wins – or loses, depending on your point of view," he said, shuffling the cards. "Aces low."

One by one, the three Grudgers reached for the cards and selected one.

"Looks like I'm the one," Arthur said, flatly as he gazed at the three of spades in his hands. Tom had the five of hearts and Paddy the king of clubs.

"Would you like to do best out of three?" Tom asked.

Arthur shook his head. "Only putting off the inevitable. It's got to be one of us. Anyway, if it doesn't work, perhaps I'm the lucky one, eh? At least I wouldn't have to starve to death. Or end up eating one of you lardy arsed buggers."

"When do you want to try it?" Sam asked.

"I doubt if I could sleep tonight knowing I was going to have to crawl along that friggin' tunnel in the morning, so I might as well do it now," Arthur said, his face deadpan. "What have I got to lose - apart from my nerve?"

"Here," Sam said to him. He went to the bar and handed him a large whisky. "Just to steady you a bit, eh?"

"Many thanks." Arthur smiled, thinly, and took a long swallow of the whisky. "Good stuff too, for once."

He looked at the galvanised tunnel, squared his shoulders, then stepped towards it. Sam handed him a heavy hammer. "A couple of hard bangs should be enough to snap the solder. If someone will help me, two of us will take a firm grip of this end of the shaft to make sure it doesn't slide forward."

"Take a bloody firm grip," Arthur said as he stooped and

stretched his hands into the tunnel, then began gingerly to crawl on all fours along it. He could feel the cold metal beneath the palms of his hands. There was an intensity to the coldness which he supposed was because the blackness surrounding it was drawing out any heat into whatever voids of nothingness there were outside.

"Are you okay?" Sam called as the old man shifted his knees into the shaft.

"Feels cold but firm," Arthur told him; he looked back with difficulty over his shoulders. "Feels as if it's resting on something solid."

"Take care," Bob told him, as he crouched down to watch him crawl foot by foot down the shaft.

Sam gritted his teeth as he and Bob held onto the shaft to make sure it didn't move. Arthur moved only slowly, not daring to jar the shaft from their fingers, conscious at every move he made of the terrifying blackness surrounding him beyond the thin metal sheets. The shaft felt so fragile he half expected it to come apart every time he moved. Even though the shaft was only twelve feet long, it took him at least five minutes to inch his way to the end. Eventually, though, he was close enough to reach out and touch it.

He pulled the hammer from under his belt.

"Two sharp blows should snap off most of the solder," Sam called to remind him.

Arthur nodded, though he knew that if the shaft wasn't long enough, if the blackness extended even further than its end, it would rush in and kill him. The thought of it made the hair prickle along his arms and neck, while his stomach tightened with apprehension into a small, icy nugget of fear.

"Two sharp blows," Arthur muttered to himself beneath his breath as he manoeuvred the hammer so that he could grip it properly and swing it far enough back in the cramped space inside the shaft to hit the plate at the end.

"Hold onto the shaft for me," Arthur shouted to Sam and Bob. "I'm going to hit it now."

He closed his eyes, tightened his grip on the hammer, made a swift, uncharacteristically sincere prayer, then swung with as much force as he could muster.

There was a dull metallic thud.

Nothing.

He gritted his teeth and swung again. Even harder this time.

One corner of the aluminium sheet pinged free and a thin shaft of light shone through the gap.

For a second Arthur stared into it, a sick feeling in the pit of his stomach, till he realised he was looking at light, however dim, not darkness.

Light!

He could barely take his eyes away from it.

"What's wrong? What's the matter?" Sam called out to him, alarmed at his stillness.

Arthur took a deep breath as relief flooded through him.

"There's light," he shouted down the shaft. "Light!"

Buoyed up by the cheers of encouragement that broke out madly behind him. Arthur swung at the metal again with determination. A couple of good, strong blows and he'd have it off. Just a couple, that was all, he thought to himself. The first blow parted the sheet from one side, and the light grew brighter. He aimed a blow at the opposite edge. Just one, he thought. Just one more blow. Make it good and hard and he'd be out of here. Out of here for good.

Back inside the pub, Sam looked at Bob as he tightened his grip on the edge of the shaft before Arthur could strike his next blow. "Nearly there," he whispered. Bob grinned, then looked down the shaft as Arthur wriggled into position, before bringing the hammer down with a resounding, echoing thud against the metal.

A dim grey light shone down the shaft as the metal fell free. It was a cold light, almost shadowy in substance. Carefully, Arthur crawled further along the shaft, till his head and shoulders were free of it. If he had expected to see any sign of the streets or houses that lay beyond the front of the pub, there was no sign of them now as he craned his neck to see as much as he could, though everything seemed to be little more than dimly-seen differing shades of grey. There was an impression of vast stone walls somewhere in the distance and high above him, as if he was in an enormous cavern. He screwed up his eyes, wishing that he had brought his glasses with him when he came to the pub, but none of his friends had ever seen him wearing them – none of them even knew that his eyesight had worsened over recent years. Out there, though, he felt sure that something moved. Something large and dark.

"Are you okay, Arthur," he heard Sam call to him as he wriggled free of the shaft and crawled onto the hard, cold surface of the stone outside. He turned around and looked back down the shaft. "It seems okay here," he called back. "But I've no idea where I am. It's not Edgebottom."

"Not Edgebottom? But how do you know?" Sam asked.

Arthur saw his face disappear for a moment as Sam discussed things with the others. He reappeared again shortly. "Hold on to your end of the shaft," Sam told him. "We're coming through."

Arthur glanced around the darkness uncertainly. "I don't know whether it's all that safe," he told him. "I keep seeing something move in the distance. Something large. I've no idea what it is, though."

"But we can't just stay here," Sam insisted.

Arthur sighed. "Okay. I'll take a hold of the shaft."

The shaft stood out a few feet from a dark, glistening mass of blackness like that surrounding the pub. He would have called it a pool, but it rose in front of him up against the side of a wall of rock. He flinched as the shaft tugged his fingers; Sam had squeezed himself into the far end of it, his pale face almost filling it as he stared at Arthur.

"Take it slow," Arthur told him. "Don't risk damaging the joins. They're not all that strong."

One by one the rest of them slowly made their way along the shaft, till all five of them eventually stood on the rough stone at

62

the end of it. Bob shivered theatrically. "It's a damn sight colder here than in the pub," he grumbled.

"You can always go back if you like," Sam said.

"I'm not sure yet whether that wouldn't be a good idea," Bob retorted. "I thought this might lead outside the pub, but God knows where it is. It doesn't ring a bell with me. It's like nowhere round Edgebottom that I've ever seen."

"Nor me," Tom said, his voice quiet, as if he felt intimidated by the vastness of the gloomy depths around them. "Oh, my gawd," he mumbled.

The rest of them followed his gaze as he stared with a look of horror into the distance.

"What is it?" Arthur asked, though he felt sure that he knew. It was that thing – that large, dark shape he had seen move when he first climbed out of the shaft. He screwed his eyes in an effort to make out what it was. It was large in the distance. Immense. Too large to be real.

The rest of them saw the creature at once, though none could have even started to describe what they saw. It was impossible for them to fix it in their gaze, as if it did not even fully exist within reality, but partially slid between dimensions even as they stared up at it. It was a Leviathan of Biblical size, perhaps octopoid, perhaps insectile, perhaps neither, or both, or many other forms of life simultaneously – or beyond all forms of life, something the like of which none of them had ever heard of or seen or imagined.

They felt fear deprive them of thought as they gazed up at it.

An impossibly long tendril reached towards them from the creature, dark, bristly, covered in rows upon rows of millions of tiny, moving suckers. Arthur shrank back against the rest of the men as it moved towards him. Sam pushed him to one side, then mindlessly scrabbled to get back as far as he could from it. Panic infected them all as they ran about against the rock face in an effort to elude the nearing limb. Paddy was the first to scream. It was a pitifully pathetic, terror-filled scream of gut-wrenching horror. The rest of them were halted for an instant as the tiny suckers transfixed themselves to Paddy's face. His arms and legs flailed in agony as he tried to tear himself free, as his face seemed to be drawn into all the suckers simultaneously, followed by the rest of his head, then shoulders. Sam felt sickened as blood erupted from all the tears that were ripped about the old man's body as it was wrenched apart into the hundreds of suckers consuming him. Sam grabbed at one of Paddy's arms, though he knew he was too late to save him. He tugged at the arm, but there was no give. The immense tendril that was drawing him violently into it was far too strong for his efforts to have any effect upon it.

More of the tendrils or octopoid limbs were emerging from the distant creature. Sam saw Tom trip as one of them soared down at him, attaching itself to his back. His screams rose in a terrible falsetto.

Bob made a bolt for the ventilation shaft to get back to the pub. But the old man was too fat and too slow to make it in time, and another tendril grasped him with its carnivorous suckers.

Was this why they had been trapped in the pub? Sam wondered. Had all this been part of some terrible plan, created by that bastard Durer?

Sam pushed Bob's writhing body to one side, then dived down the shaft. The brighter light of the pub was ahead of him, and he moved with reckless speed down the shaft towards it, conscious of the possibility that one of the tendrils and its deadly suckers might only be inches away behind him.

He slithered out of the end into the pub, scrabbling at the ground to tug himself as fast as he could from the shaft. The metallic structure was moving behind him, and he knew that something else was inside it. A scream was stuck in the back of his throat as he stared at the exit, his fists clenched in a useless gesture of defence, when Arthur thrust himself out of the shaft.

"Help me!" the old man shouted. And Sam saw the thick tip of the tendril that had attached itself to one of his feet emerge from the shaft as Arthur crawled across the floor into the pub.

Blood burst from his leg as the suckers commenced their terrible, relentless, irresistible work on him, consuming him even as he struggled to get as far as he could from the shaft. "HELP ME!"

Sam pushed himself to his feet and ran behind the bar into the kitchen. He tugged out the cutlery drawer by the sink. Then ran back into the pub, a carving knife clenched in one fist.

Without hesitation he hacked at the tendril, but the thing was so tough it was like trying to cut through seasoned mahogany. Sharp though the blade was, it barely scratched the surface of the tendril.

"Sam!" Arthur screamed at him, the foot and ankle of his left leg a ruin. "Do something, for Christ's sake!"

Sam threw the knife to one side.

"What can I do?" he asked him, agitated and frightened. He kicked at the end of the shaft, then on an impulse he reached down and tugged it. He felt it come free as he pulled the far end that was still in the cavern back into the darkness. The tendril, still trapped inside it, disappeared in an instant as darkness filled it. The rest of the tendril flopped onto the floor, falling away from Arthur's ruptured foot, its severed end oozing thick black fluids that hissed and bubbled on the floor of the pub.

Sam dragged Arthur away from the tendril and up onto a chair near the bar. He wrapped a towel round his injured foot. The old man moaned, but he was still conscious.

"What's happening to us, Sam?" the old man asked.

"I don't know for sure," Sam said. "But I intend to find out." He looked towards the stairs.

"What're you going to do?"

"Something I should have thought of days ago," Sam muttered.

Clenching his fists, Sam strode up the stairs till he stood in the doorway to Albert Durer's bedroom. He stared in at the painted pentacle and circle and the dead rat nailed in the centre of them. He stepped into the pentacle and kicked the stiffened carcass from the nails pinning it to the floorboards. He then kicked at the painted lines and curves and obscure symbols, scuffing them with the hard leather soles of his boots. He went out into the upstairs kitchen and found a knife. Back in Durer's bedroom he set to work scraping and slicing as much as he could of the pentacle away. Then he went to the sash window, pulled back its curtains and pushed up the bottom of the window frame. Outside, the ominous, threatening blackness loomed before him. He reached for the book on the dresser. For a second he looked down at its stained, old pages, with their obscure, thickly printed lines of writing and strange drawings. Then he raised the book and threw it with as much force as he could muster out into the darkness.

He sank to his knees. There was nothing else he could think of to do. After this, all there was left was to return to the bar and give what help he could to Arthur. A feeling of helplessness seeped through him as he raised his head and looked at the window – through which the first rays of dawn were starting to emerge from above the dark grey roofs to the east.

No one amongst all the scores of police and local and regional government officials who had gathered about the outside of the pub over the last few days was able to give Sam any reason for the "Strange Anomaly" (as they termed it) that had isolated the Potter's Wheel from the rest of the normal world. Nevertheless, it was only a matter of minutes before Arthur was whisked away in an ambulance to the nearest hospital to have his injuries treated, while Sam showed a small group of the most senior investigators about the pub.

In the months that followed the reality of what happened became blurred through layers of "official" explanations, denials, claims that the whole thing was some kind of hoax, and an inability of the two survivors from inside the pub to grasp just what had happened to them, as it began to seem, as they looked back on it, as a strange kind of dream or nightmare or, as some experts suggested to them, mass hallucination.

Of his late lodger, Albert Durer, Sam never heard anything more. The odd man appeared to have disappeared completely as if he had never existed. That he had almost certainly used a false name was soon pointed out, when someone mentioned that he must have taken it from the German painter Albrecht Durer, dead for over four hundred years.

"He'd wish he'd been dead that long too if I ever get my hands on him," Sam would mutter to himself when well in his cups. But he knew there was little chance of that. If he was still alive, "Durer" would be well away from here by now, his mischief done. Though whether he would do what he'd tried to do in the Potter's Wheel elsewhere... Sam shuddered at the thought. Especially when Arthur hobbled into the pub at night for enough drinks to help him sleep. Then the two of them would talk into the early hours of the morning of those terrible events and marvel that even two of them had survived.

THE FRAGILE MASK ON HIS FACE

It had been a long night and Helen was glad to get away when the class finally ended. She neatly stacked her notes together, then slid them inside her briefcase.

"Do you fancy going for a drink on the way home?" Joyce asked, her own notes rolled in a rubber band and stuffed into her coat pocket.

Helen wasn't sure. It was Thursday and it was a normal workday tomorrow.

"One drink won't make you ill," Joyce insisted, almost mind-reading the reasons for Helen's indecision. "And don't tell me, after tonight's session, you don't feel like having something to help you unwind."

"I had thought of a cup of hot chocolate," Helen said, but she could feel herself giving way. Joyce's bouncy enthusiasm was almost irresistible and a sure tonic for any tiredness she might have felt a few moments before.

"One round. That's all. No more than two anyway," Joyce said, flashing a smile. "Besides, it's so cold tonight, you need something to warm you up."

The Potter's Wheel was only just off the town centre and reassuringly busy midweek. Just the usual suspects, Helen thought as she took a seat at one of the tables by the wall, while Joyce strode over to the bar. A boisterous group of old men occupied one window table, itself crowded out with full and half full pints of beer. Throughout the rest of the pub there was a dense scattering of singletons, quietly drinking their chosen solace, while a group of pool players were shouting and laughing in the next room.

"Do you think they picked this particular shade of brown so you couldn't see the nicotine stains?" Joyce asked as she deposited their drinks on the table, then shed her heavy coat. Beneath she wore a thick jumper that could have out-rivalled Joseph's coat of many colours.

"Could you not find anything more startling?" Helen asked, pretending that her eyes were being dazzled. "It was distracting enough in class."

"I'll have you know my mum made this for me and she has impeccable taste."

They broke out in laughter, then sipped their drinks, a lager for Joyce and a gin and tonic for Helen.

"Oh, oh, there's Goggle Eyes giving you the once over again."

Although, with a break from college over Christmas, it was nearly a month since they last came into the Potter's Wheel, Helen still remembered the pale young man with the goatee beard, a worn corduroy jacket and dark, curly hair, whose eyes always seemed to keep glancing their way, though he had never made any other indication of noticing their presence as he sat, slowly drinking his glass of cider.

"That's cruel," Helen said.

"You're joking. If they're not the closest things you've ever seen to goggle eyes on a man…"

Helen shook her head, though she had to admit it was an accurate description.

"I just hope he never hears you."

Joyce grinned and took another sip of her drink. "Fat chance of that with those old guys over there. They make more noise than a pack of unruly school kids."

Laughing and shouting and arguing with each other with the boisterous camaraderie born of decades of familiarity, the old men were as much a part of the pub as its outdated décor.

"Anyway, I don't think it's a good idea to make fun of him, even between ourselves. There's no saying how much he might pick up, even without hearing us."

Joyce snorted. "You're a real little scaredy cat, Helen. Anyway, he's as far through as a tram ticket, even if he did get upset."

Helen felt like saying that this wasn't the point, but it would have been wasted on Joyce, who would only be encouraged to make even more outrageous comments about him if she persisted.

"I'm surprised Tony wasn't here to meet you after class," Helen said, to change the subject.

"Tony's history now, Helen. History." There was a sneer that jarred with her humour a moment before, and Helen wondered just how historical Tony was.

"You've argued?"

"You could put it like that." Joyce pulled out a slightly crumpled pack of cigarettes and lit one. "See this? See the state of it? I've tried to give up half a dozen times since I told him to fuck off. I've fished this pack out of the bin three times already." She glanced around at the young man in the corduroy jacket. "Seen enough?" she snapped at him irritably.

"Joyce!" Helen admonished. "Keep your voice down."

There was already a lull amongst the old men, and Helen felt as if every eye in the pub was on them.

"I think I'll settle with just one drink," she said, taking a quick gulp of her gin and tonic, and tried not to cough as the harsh liquid caught in her throat.

"Helen, I'm sorry." Joyce touched her wrist. "It's just that I'm still a bit raw about the bastard."

"That's all right. But you shouldn't let your feelings about him make you lash out at other people."

Joyce nodded. "I know. I said I'm sorry." She smiled wryly. "Am I forgiven?"

For a moment Helen wondered. Joyce's mood swings tonight were catching her off balance and she really didn't feel up to it. The accountancy lesson had already taken its toll on her, what with that and worrying about the exams looming ahead of her at Easter and all the revision she would have to do, listening to Joyce's outbursts were too much just now.

"You're forgiven," she said. "Of course you are. Though

there's really nothing to forgive in the first place. But I really am tired."

"One more drink," Joyce insisted. "I'll get it. Just one. Then we'll go to the bus station together. It'll be safer that way."

Which was true. There had been too many attacks against women walking the streets at night by themselves, even in built-up areas, for her to feel easy about heading for the bus station from here on her own.

"Another gin and tonic?" Joyce asked.

Helen nodded. It would help her relax, if nothing else, she thought, as the effects of her first drink began to flow through her. She glanced over at "Goggle Eyes", feeling guilty as the nickname Joyce had bestowed on him automatically came to mind, especially when she caught him looking towards her. His large, round, slightly protuberant eyes instantly turned downwards to stare at his drink, and she wondered if she caught a faint trace of a blush on his pallid cheeks. He reminded her of a very young, lightly bearded Peter Lorre; his strange eyes, far from being repellent, were oddly exotic.

"Here we are," Joyce announced, perhaps a trifle too cheerfully as she once more deposited drinks on their table.

As they talked Helen suspected that, given the chance, Joyce wanted to linger even longer in the pub, but it was nearly ten and Helen had a twenty-minute ride ahead of her even after they reached the bus station. As soon as she had finished her gin and tonic she told Joyce that she really had to be going now.

Joyce reluctantly placed her own emptied glass on the table.

"You sure?" she asked, but Helen was already putting on her coat.

Outside, the cold had become even more bitter than before, and Helen knew that winter had well and truly arrived.

"Hope it doesn't snow again," Joyce moaned as they ducked their heads into the wind. "Perhaps we should have rung for a taxi."

"I can't afford taxis. Besides, it's only five minutes to the bus station."

Joyce suddenly stopped. "Bugger and damnation!"

"What's the matter?" Helen turned her back to the wind to face her.

"I must have left my notes from tonight in the pub."

"Are you certain?"

"Positive. They were in my coat pocket. They must have fallen out while I was putting it on." An extra strong gust of wind howled around them, bringing icy cold through every gap in their clothing.

"I'll nip back for them. I'll only be a few minutes. I'll catch you up on the way to the bus station."

Helen looked down the long, deserted street, with its closed shops, sheltering behind galvanised steel shutters daubed with graffiti. Flakes of snow were beginning to spin across the road, adding to the brown smear of slush spread across it.

"I can come back with you," Helen offered. But Joyce shook her head. "I'll run and catch you up."

With that she began to hurry back to the pub, its windows beckoning with their comforting glow against the darkness.

Turning back into the wind, Helen again ducked her head against it.

Typical of Joyce to desert her like this, she decided. It wouldn't have surprised her if her friend still had her notes on her and was using their alleged loss as an excuse to get back to the pub for another drink and to order a taxi, never mind that this left Helen out here on her own. Feeling angry, Helen strode on faster, determined to reach the bus station well ahead of Joyce, even if she did intend to try and catch up and it wasn't all a lie.

She had almost reached the bus station when the car passed her. The snow had become heavier in the last few minutes, and was sticking to the ground. Slush from beneath the car's tyres hissed through the air, striking her legs in icy lumps. She stopped, gasping at the shock of it. Bloody fool, she thought, angry at the driver for speeding past so close to the kerb. She looked up at it. And thought she saw Joyce's face pressed to the rear windscreen, looking back at her. But most of the glass was already covered in snow and she could have been mistaken. It wasn't even a taxi and she could think of no reason why Joyce should have got a lift in someone's car, especially from the Potter's Wheel, where they were hardly even on nodding terms with any of the regulars.

Next Thursday, though, Helen was disturbed when Joyce failed to turn up at night school. This was a crucial time for both of them, with only a couple of months to go before their exams. When the lesson had finished she asked Henry Hanshaw, their tutor, a stiff, thin-haired academic with a perpetually miserable expression on his face, if Joyce had rung in, but he told her he had no idea why Joyce hadn't come here tonight. Ringing in wasn't a requirement. They weren't schoolchildren. They or their employers had paid for this course and as far as Henry Hanshaw was concerned it was up to them if they came or not.

Stifling her irritation at his infuriating manner, Helen took out her mobile and rang Joyce's number, but there was no answer. Instead she was diverted to Joyce's answer phone facility. She left a brief message.

"Hope you are okay. Missed you tonight. If you need any help with this week's lesson, give me a ring."

She put her phone away and strode out of the austere college building. Last week's snow still lay on the ground in glaciated rucks, with ominously glistening patches of ice, which Helen gingerly avoided.

The Potter's Wheel was only a few minutes out of her way to the bus station and, though she knew Joyce was unlikely to be there, for some reason Helen felt the need for a drink before going home.

As she settled in the pub's comforting warmth, Helen remembered that she let Joyce borrow her mobile to ring her boyfriend, Tony, a few weeks ago, the battery of her own phone having gone flat. Helen looked up her record of dialled calls and scrolled down them till she found the one that was probably his. Suspecting that there may have been a reconciliation between

74

them, which could account for Joyce's absence tonight, Helen rang Tony's number. A few seconds later she heard his familiar voice.

"Tony Farr."

"Hi, Tony, it's Helen Taylor. I'm trying to get hold of Joyce. You haven't seen her lately, have you?"

"Joyce?" Tony hesitated, as if embarrassed. "I haven't been in touch with Joyce for over a week. She's not answering her phone. She has it on divert, which I think is her way of telling me that she doesn't want to talk things over." If embarrassed to start with, his voice had very quickly adopted a tone of being aggrieved.

Ignoring this, Helen said: "She should have been at our accountancy class tonight, but she didn't turn up. That's why I'm ringing. I wondered if you guys might have made up or something."

"Fat chance of that," Tony responded petulantly.

"I'm sorry you've had an argument. I know it's none of my business, but I was sad to hear about it."

"Thanks."

"I'm beginning to get worried about Joyce. She didn't need to put her phone on divert to avoid talking to you. She could just cancel your calls when she sees who they're from. Anyway, she's not responded yet to the message I left half an hour ago."

Tony paused for a moment, probably collecting his thoughts, she supposed.

"I don't know what to suggest. I did go round to her place earlier this week, but she wasn't in. Or, if she was, she wouldn't answer her door. Though there weren't any lights on."

Helen could imagine him standing there, minute after minute, ringing the doorbell, then banging on its panels. Patience had never been one of Tony's virtues from what she knew about him.

"Perhaps she's staying with her mother," Helen suggested finally.

"Perhaps," he replied. "But I tried there as well. And, unless she's got her mother to lie for her, she's not there either."

All of which was beginning to make Helen feel distinctly uneasy. She remembered the face she glimpsed in the back of the car that doused her with slush a week ago on her way to the station. Had it been Joyce's face she saw in the back of it after all, she wondered. She preferred not to dwell too much on the expression she seemed to remember on the woman's face. As she looked back on it now she could not understand how she had failed to recognise the fear and panic that had stared back at her.

"What are you going to do now?" Tony asked. For the first time there wasn't a trace of anger, resentment or self justification in his voice. Just worry.

"I'll ring her mum myself. I don't think she would have lied for Joyce. But even if she did, she wouldn't have any reason to lie to me."

"Will you ring me back when you've spoken?" Tony asked.

Helen smiled, despite her fears. "Okay."

After Tony had given her the number for Joyce's mother she rang off and called it.

"Mrs Wainwright? It's Helen Taylor. Joyce's friend."

The woman who answered sounded cautious, though that was probably because of the lateness of the hour. Only now did Helen realise it was nearly ten o'clock.

"Is anything wrong? Joyce hasn't had an accident, has she?"

"Not so far as I know. That's why I'm ringing. She missed her lesson at college tonight and isn't answering her phone, so I thought she might be staying with you."

"She's not staying with me, dear. In fact, I haven't heard from her for over a week. I was starting to get worried. She usually rings every day or so to see how I am."

After promising to get Joyce to phone her mum the moment she got in touch with her, Helen sat pensively for a short while, then finished her drink. She remembered that she had promised to ring Tony back, and decided that she would get another drink, then call him. At the bar she asked the landlord if he remembered her friend calling back into the pub again last week because she'd lost some papers.

The landlord scratched one ear for a moment in thought. "Curly red hair, wearing a very, *very* colourful jumper?" he asked.

Helen said that was her.

"I remember her, yes. She came back here all right. All in a-flutter, she was. Found her papers, though. They were on the floor right where you'd been sitting."

"Did she leave again straight away?"

"Probably. But I can't remember, sweetheart. There were a few people leaving about that time. Something good must have been coming on telly that night. Regular little exodus, it was."

"I don't suppose it's any good asking if you remember if she left by herself?"

The landlord beamed. "'Fraid not, my love. I was too busy with that gang over there." He nodded to the old men sat by the window. "They were ordering in another round about that time and it was all hands to the pumps, if you get my drift."

Collecting her drink, Helen returned to her table. "Goggle Eyes" was here again, drinking his cider, the glass nearly full. Though he never seemed to finish it, from what she could recall. Just took small sips, as if he didn't really care for it at all and only had it because you had to have a drink of some sort to be here, she pondered, before her thoughts inevitably returned to Joyce.

She took out her mobile and called Tony. He answered straight away as if he had been waiting. Which he probably had been, Helen thought.

"Any news?" he asked.

"Her mum's not heard from her for over a week. She's worried herself, as Joyce normally keeps in regular touch with her."

"Oh, God," Tony moaned, and she wondered if he was feeling guilty now about whatever it was that made them row. "Do you think we should contact the police?" he asked.

"I don't know," Helen said. "Would they take any notice after only a week?"

"I'll ring her office in the morning," Tony said. "If she's not been to work and hasn't rung in sick, then I think we should go to the police anyway."

Helen agreed. "Till then I don't suppose there's much more we can do."

Afterwards she stared for a few minutes at her drink, wondering if perhaps Joyce had met someone else on the rebound and was spending time with them. From what she knew of her, there was always a possibility of that. A very distinct possibility, she thought, which was one reason why she was reluctant to involve the police just yet.

"Excuse me, is your friend not going to be with you tonight?"

Helen looked up, startled. It was "Goggle Eyes". He had risen from his table and was stood next to her, contrary to her thoughts a few moments ago, having actually drained his pint. Holding the empty glass in one hand, he was on his way to the bar.

"I'm afraid not," Helen said after a pause that seemed to go on a little too long as she tried to collect her thoughts.

The young man nodded, as if absorbing the information, then took a step further towards the bar, paused, and said: "I couldn't get you a drink, could I? I see you've nearly finished."

Flustered at the unexpected offer, Helen said: "I wouldn't say no," though she regretted accepting almost at once. But it was too late. By then "Goggle Eyes" was already at the bar.

"I asked Bob for the same drink you had last time – Gin and tonic, he said – if that's all right," the young man told her a few moments later when he returned.

"You really shouldn't have," Helen said.

"No problem. You look as if you're worried about something. Perhaps this will help cheer you up."

"Thank you, but I don't think it will, really. I'm worried about my friend. She's gone missing and no one seems to know where she is."

"That's bad," the young man said. He held out one hand. "My name's Mat Denton."

Helen took his hand lightly. It felt cold and soft. "Helen. Helen Taylor."

He smiled, looking slightly embarrassed.

"I hope you don't think I'm being presumptive, offering you a drink like that. But I feel like I almost know you, with you and your friend coming in here every week or so over the past year."

"I suppose we have become sort of familiar faces here," Helen admitted, uncertainly.

"Sort of." Mat took a tiny sip of his cider. "This friend of yours…?"

"Joyce."

"When was the last time you saw her?"

"In here. Last Thursday. We were on our way to the bus station when she remembered leaving something here and returned. She said she would catch me up a few minutes later, but she didn't."

"I was in here last Thursday," Mat said, though Helen already remembered this. She also remembered Joyce being unnecessarily rude to him.

"You don't know if she spoke to anyone when she returned, do you?"

Mat thought for a moment. "It was very busy just then. The old Grudgers, that lot over there," he added, indicating the old men, "were ordering a fresh round of drinks, and that always causes bedlam. And a few people were leaving about then, though I don't know why."

"The landlord thinks it was because something was starting on TV in a short while."

"Could have been, though I wouldn't know. I never watch television myself."

Helen added one more item to her list of oddities about him. He was the only man she could remember meeting who actually claimed that he never watched TV. What an odd thing to claim, she thought, unless he spent most of his nights here in the

79

Potter's Wheel taking miniscule sips of his cider.

Somehow Helen managed to pass the next ten minutes in a disjointed form of conversation with Mat, till she finished her drink.

"Would you like another," Mat asked, but Helen was prepared and said: "No. I really must be on my way." She reached for her briefcase. "I have work tomorrow and it will take me at least an hour to get home."

Outside it was cold, miserable and quiet, her footsteps echoing back at her as she headed through the town centre to the bus station. She was barely halfway there, though, when she heard her mobile chime, telling her that she had just received a text message. For a moment she was undecided whether to wait till she reached the bus station before checking out what it was, but ahead was the lit doorway of Marks and Spencer, and she decided to stand there for a moment to read it.

She was surprised to see the message was from Joyce.

"hi. sorry u r worrying about me. i'm ok. meet you in a few minutes. i'll pick you up in my car. i'll explain all then. joyce."

Meet you in a few minutes? Helen looked up and down the street. There were several cars moving, but which was hers? In fact, Helen hadn't been aware till now that Joyce even had one. It was something she had never mentioned before and had always gone home from college by bus. Anyway, Helen thought, how does she know where I'll be? Or had she been watching the Potter's Wheel? Which hardly made sense.

Undecided, Helen wondered whether to ignore the message and continue on her way to the bus station. So long as Joyce was all right that was all she was really bothered about. She wasn't interested in meeting her, certainly not at this time of night, when she was more concerned in getting home to her flat and a relaxing warm drink curled up in front of the fire, with perhaps an hour or so of watching TV to unwind, before going to bed. Why should she want to meet Joyce now to hear why she had not been to college tonight?

A large, dark car pulled up alongside her. Its passenger door swung open. Inside she could just make out Joyce's face at the steering wheel. She looked pale, almost peaky, though that could have been because of the gloominess of the car, lit only by a small white light that came on above the windscreen when the door opened.

"Come on. Jump in," Joyce barked, her voice harsh as if she had a sore throat.

When Helen hesitated, Joyce added: "It's getting cold in here. Please hurry. I'll drive you home while we talk."

An icy gust of wind, billowing down the high street and striking deep through Helen's coat, decided her, and she ducked her head beneath the door frame and let herself fall back onto the passenger seat, her briefcase on her lap. Almost immediately, as soon as Helen closed the door behind her, Joyce accelerated away from the kerb, driving quickly through town.

It was only then that Helen realised there was someone slumped on the seat behind her. She looked round as much as she could. In the intermittent light cast into the car she was surprised to see Tony Farr. His mouth jerked into a sort of smile when he saw her look at him.

"Have you guys' made up?" Helen asked, disturbed at the silence that had fallen over everyone in the car.

"Later," Joyce said.

Helen stared at her as the car turned onto a road that would take them up onto the moors above the town. Darkness loomed ahead of the car as the street lights petered out along the winding road to become randomly intermittent.

"Which way are we heading?" she asked Joyce. "Is this a short cut?"

A large farmhouse rose in silhouette against the pale, snow-laden clouds that dominated the sky. Joyce drove down a rough path that branched off the road towards it, drawing up a moment later on a snow-streaked cobblestone yard.

"What is this place?" Helen demanded. "And why have we stopped here?"

Joyce ignored her as she opened her door and climbed out of

the car. Behind her, Helen heard Tony heave himself out onto the yard too, standing beside the car like an indistinct shadow.

For a moment Helen hesitated. Though she had known Joyce long enough to trust her – and had even grown to like Tony from what she had seen of him – there was something about the two of them now that disturbed her. Tony looked ill. He looked worse than ill. He looked like he seriously needed to see a doctor. His face had the grey pallor of someone with an ominously critical heart condition. Indeed, as the wind buffeted him, he rested against the side of the car as if it was too much effort to stand unaided.

"This way," Joyce said, and she led them towards the main door into the farmhouse. It swung open as she pushed it. "Inside," she went on, leading the way. A light came on in the hallway; Helen stared into the large, unfurnished room. Opposite, a flight of stairs rose into darkness. The walls were covered in old, patterned paper, stained with huge patches of damp; much of it looked like fungus. There was an overpoweringly dense smell of mould, dry rot and vermin, and Helen felt sure she would be sick if she was forced to stand inside. But Tony had moved up even closer now, pressing against her, and she stumbled forwards, up the worn flagstone steps and into the hallway, almost gagging on the smell.

Joyce, though, seemed unaffected by it. Or was she? Helen seemed to detect a change in her friend's face as she strode across the threadbare, old-fashioned carpet that only partially covered the floorboards, her heels thudding across them. She turned and faced Helen and Tony. There was a mark around the edge of her face that Helen had not noticed before, like a ragged line. Their eyes met. Joyce's looked strange, almost milky, old and oddly shrivelled. She felt suddenly squeamish as Joyce reached up to touch the line. A fingernail seemed to catch beneath it. Then slowly, deliberately she began to peal the skin from her face. It came away with disgusting ease.

"Joyce!" Helen called out, sickened at the sight of her friend's face clutched like a flimsy, cheap Halloween mask in her fingers, till she realised that the face underneath wasn't the disfigured remnants of Joyce's at all, but the blood-blotched face of Mat Denton.

For a moment she felt utter revulsion, then everything seemed to swim before her eyes. Her sense of balance deserted her and she was aware suddenly of falling forwards, of reaching out to protect herself as the floor seemed to tip towards her.

And the cold, hard, snow-covered paving stones jarred against her arms and knees and made her cry out in pain as she slithered across them.

"Are you all right, lass?"

She looked up. Speckles of light danced in front of everything as an intense feeling of nausea washed through her and she felt the urge to be sick.

"Did you slip on the ice?"

The man's voice sounded friendly enough. An old man's voice. She looked up as he carefully took hold of one arm and helped her to her feet. The light from the window display in the Marks and Spencer store next to them looked comfortingly normal, as Helen looked around herself in disbelief. The old man held a walking stick in one hand as he gripped on to her arm with the other, a look of concern on his face.

"You took a right tumble then, lass. Have you hurt yourself?"

"I think I'm all right," Helen said, though her voice still sounded distant and she had a strange feeling of disorientation.

Just then her mobile rang. Clumsily, the palms of her hands scuffed raw by the paving stones, she fumbled through her pockets as the old man stood back and watched her with concern.

She saw before she answered her phone that the call was from Tony Farr. An image of him, grey faced and mute, stood outside the semi-derelict farmhouse, came to mind, of the strange dream or hallucination that had come over her when she fell.

"Hello, Tony," she murmured, still feeling shaken.

"Are you all right, Helen?" His voice sounded concerned, even nervous.

"I think so. Why? What made you ask?"

There was a pause. "I don't know. I just had the oddest experience. I thought you were in danger. Sounds stupid, I know."

"Did you have some kind of a waking dream?" she asked.

The pause this time was even longer. The old man who had helped her nodded, then started to walk away, carefully shuffling his feet across the icy pavement.

"How did you know?" Tony asked.

It was a question Helen could barely understand herself. Why should he have had a dream? What made her ask? And what made him ring? The more she thought about it the less sense it made.

"I just fell," she told him. "Slipped on the ice, I suppose. And had a bizarre dream about Joyce."

"That she came for you in a car?"

For a moment Helen wondered if the dream had really ended, if this was still a part of it, if she had not woken up at all. But the pain in her hands and knees was enough to convince her that this was real. Even if she was asleep this would have been enough in itself to waken her.

"What's happened to her, Tony?"

"Where are you?" he asked. "I'll come and meet you."

Feeling that this was some weird kind of *deja vu*, with Tony replacing Joyce this time, she told him where she was.

"Stay there," he said. "I'll be with you in less than ten minutes."

He drew up even before the first five minutes had passed, his car screeching to a standstill on the gritted road. He looked tussled and edgy when he came round to help her across the pavement to the passenger door, concerned at the scuffs on her hands and knees.

"I'll take you home as soon as we've finished," he said. "But I'd like to take a diversion first."

"Up onto the moors?" Helen asked, her voice quiet. "To the farmhouse?"

"If it exists," Tony said flatly. "This sounds nuts to me. But the dream seemed so real. So oddly real."

"Our dream, you mean," Helen said.

"That's even more stupid." Even though they had not discussed their dream in detail, they both knew they had experienced the same, impossible though they knew this was.

Tony drove carefully. The moorland road had not been gritted for days and shone with a menacingly black glossiness in the headlamps. Farmhouses up here were widely scattered and lonely, grim-looking buildings, surrounded by lines of dry-stone walls and snow-covered hedgerows.

"There it is," Helen said, no trace of excitement or enthusiasm in her voice. She had been hoping against hope that they would find nothing here, that their nightmare had been nothing more than a dream. But there was no mistaking the dark, isolated, box-like building.

Tony nodded in recognition, then carefully drove down the side road towards it. He flipped open the glove compartment and took out a torch. "Are you game?" he asked. "Or would you prefer to wait in the car?"

Helen did not hesitate. "I'd be more scared waiting for you by myself."

He smiled, briefly, then climbed out. They approached the farmhouse gingerly. The icy cobblestone yard in front of it was hazard enough, even without the strong winds that buffeted them. But it was more than just this that made them walk slowly. There was an ominous presence about the unlit building, an aura that disquietened both of them, and Helen wondered if it would not have been better to have left this till daylight, perhaps after ringing the police. Although how they could explain their interest in this place without mentioning their dream she was not sure. And just how that would go down with the police she could well imagine.

At the door Tony hesitated, then he rapped on it. The sound

seemed to echo through the hollow emptiness of the building. When there was no response, he rapped once more, then tried the handle.

"Locked."

With a grunt, he strode over to the nearest window and shone his torch inside. Satisfied that the place was empty, he returned to the door, took a step back, then kicked it hard with the flat sole of his foot immediately below the lock. The door thudded open explosively, bouncing against its overtaxed hinges.

The musty mixture of mould, decay and rat droppings was unmistakeable.

"How can it be so similar?" Helen murmured, as Tony shone his torch into the unlit interior. There was the staircase and the damp-raddled wallpaper, with its patches of evil-looking fungi, and the worn-out scraps of carpet that barely covered the old floorboards. It was not just similar to what they had seen in their dream, it was identical. The only element missing was Joyce.

Tony led the way inside, his footsteps hollow on the floorboards. Helen shivered. Apart from the wind, it was virtually as cold inside the farmhouse as outside on the moors.

"No one lives here," she murmured, dispiritedly, wishing she was home. "Look at the ice on the walls. There's been no heating in this place all winter."

Tony nodded. "Let's explore. If we find nothing, what have we lost?"

Though she was uneasy about this, Helen nevertheless fell in step behind him as he moved to the nearest door. It opened stiffly, its hinges frozen. Like the hallway, this room was empty apart from cobwebs, dust, patches of mould and the inevitable scattering of rat droppings. Once started, though, they continued to move about the house, going from room to room on the ground floor, including the kitchen, with its stone sink half full of green slime and broken crockery, and cupboards littered with mouldering packets of food, abandoned here when the last inhabitants moved out what must have been years ago.

"We're wasting our time," Helen grumbled, feeling the cold numbing her hands and feet.

"Then why did we dream about it?" Tony insisted, gritting his teeth. "There must be some reason. There must."

Returning to the hallway, he started up the stairs. The landing above wavered in the torchlight; its banister rails cast elongated shadows across the high ceiling.

"Are you sure?" Helen asked. The steps creaked beneath her feet and she was sure she could smell dry rot in the air. If the floor gave way beneath them and they were badly injured they would be dead from exposure long before anyone found them here. But Tony climbed the stairs with a determination she could only attempt at mimicking. On the landing Tony paused just long enough to scan the line of doors facing them. Some were partially open, revealing rooms just as empty as those downstairs. One at the end, though, was different. It was the main bedroom at the front of the house. The door was shut fast and had a large, inverted cross painted on its varnished panels in bright red. Tony turned to Helen, his face grim. It was almost too obvious, and Helen was tempted to urge him to wait, but Tony's eyes were full of rage as he looked again at the door, its crudely painted symbol taunting him. Abruptly he suddenly levelled the torch and marched down the landing so quickly that Helen had to run to catch up.

He gripped the handle and thrust the door violently open.

The large, gloomy, dank room beyond seemed to change shape and size as the torch beam darted about it, picking out the strange symbols painted all over the bare floorboards and about its walls. Hundreds of partially used candles were littered about the edge of the room, surrounded by hardened rivulets of melted wax. But dominating the floor was an immense five-pointed star painted inside a crudely outlined chalk circle. Within the pentacle lay the body of a woman, her ankles and wrists bound with rope to metal rings fixed to the floorboards.

Tony grunted with horror as if he was about to be sick.

Dried blood had soaked into the floorboards around the

woman's head. Her face, which had been savagely cut away, was an unrecognisable horror of darkened, decaying flesh, sinews, cartilage and sliced blood vessels that lay exposed across the front of the skull. Beyond the pentacle, heaped against the wall, was a pile of discarded clothes, amongst them a dirtied, brightly coloured jumper. By then, though, Helen had already recognised the curly red hair of her friend, spread amongst the dried blood surrounding the disfigured head.

This time, when reaction swept in, Helen was violently sick. Her stomach heaved again and again till there was nothing left but bile, and her throat felt scoured by stomach acids.

"The bloody, fucking, murderous bastard!" Tony grated in a voice stretched taut by emotion.

He stepped into the room. From within it, as if moving out from behind an invisible barrier, a figure emerged on the other side of the pentacle, though Helen would have sworn that a moment before there was no one there. She gasped with horror as she recognised Joyce's face, stretched like a very old waxen mask across that of the man, whose dark, distinctive corduroy jacket she recognised at once – as she did the swollen, glittering eyes that gazed out at her from between the eyelids of her friend's dead face.

Tony crouched as the figure moved towards him, too late to avoid the hammer in Mat Denton's fist. Helen watched as Denton raised it high into the air, high enough for the torchlight to pick out the matted strands of hair that were stuck to its head. Then it swung down, swiftly, bounced off Tony's upraised arm with a crack which she knew was a bone breaking, and Tony cried out in pain.

"Oh, my God!" Helen whimpered, too shocked to move.

From somewhere close she seemed to hear a voice call to her: "But I warned you. *I warned you!*"

Mat Denton, the dead face wrinkling across his own hidden face as his mouth twisted in a snarl, moved in on Tony as he swung the hammer down again. And again. With savage, resounding blows that beat down the weak defence of Tony's arms, then pummelled his head.

"Joyce!" Helen cried out, though she did not know why – except for the voice that had sounded so much like her friend's. "*Joyce!*"

It was then that another figure seemed to flicker within the room. Mat Denton, distracted, looked round, the fragile mask on his face becoming even more wrinkled, becoming even less like that of Joyce as he suddenly started to back away from Tony. The raw-faced apparition took a step towards him and Mat took a further step away from it. Which was when Helen heard the floorboards give way as the smell of dry rot became more intense. Mat lost his balance as his feet crashed through the weakened wood. Dust motes rose into the air around him, grey with fungus. The translucent, faceless female figure reached out towards him, and it was as if its added weight, if such a thing had any weight at all, was enough to destroy what solidity the floorboards still had. Mat Denton cried out as, with a resounding crash, he fell through the floorboards, and through the fragile plaster and ceiling paper beneath. His arms reached out in a desperate attempt to stay his fall, but it was too late, and Helen watched in stunned silence as he gazed towards her before disappearing into the room below.

Helen was on her feet in an instant. She rushed to Tony to pull him back away from the hole and onto the safety of the landing. He was barely conscious; blood streamed down his face from where the hammer had hit him, but he was still breathing.

"We have to get out of here," she whispered to him. There was no certainty that the fall into the room below would have been enough to hurt Mat Denton seriously enough to make him harmless, and she half expected to see his plaster-covered figure return up the stairs towards them. Which was when she heard the scream. The seemingly endless, high-pitched scream of unutterable agony and terror.

Helen gripped Tony's shoulders and began to drag him with desperation along the landing towards the stairs. They had to get out of here. Get back to his car. Get out of this place completely.

At the stairs she halted. All was silent now apart from Tony's stertorous breathing.

How she managed to manhandle Tony's body down the stairs, step by step, without injuring him worse than he already was, she was afterwards unable to recall properly. Most of her consciousness was concentrated too much on listening for Mat Denton. But, eventually, what seemed like hours later, she reached the hallway. The door into the next room was still open. Lying there, amidst the debris, was Mat Denton's body.

Whether it was rage or fear that he might come round while she was still struggling to get Tony to the car across the frozen cobblestone yard outside, Helen knew she had to make sure that Denton was either dead or too badly injured to threaten them again.

It was only after she had seen him that the full horror of it all hit her. Mat Denton was all but dead. But she doubted that his fall from the room above had been what killed him, though she had no intention of staying there long enough to find out. Somehow she managed to get Tony back into his car, driving off as quickly as she could away from the farm and the moors and on into town, where she headed for the hospital. Fortunately, the blows on Tony's head had been enough to blur his memories of that night's events, and she was able to fabricate a story of him being attacked in town by a gang of thugs.

She never returned to the farmhouse. And it was months before anyone ventured there and found what remained of Mat Denton's body: by then, time, decay and the ravenous appetites of the local vermin had done much to remove the full horror of what she saw that night. Of how his face had been ripped away from his head by what she knew must have been human nails; leaving only a red, raw ruin around his staring, barely living eyes - eyes which stared up in stark, paralysed terror, even in the daytime.

THE TRUE SPIRIT

"Grudge End, in the moorland town of Edgebottom, was once sorely known as a haven for witchcraft and the darkest forms of sorcery. It is common knowledge that Helen Hayhurst, Mother Whittle and Alice Cropper were hanged at Lancaster in 1612 for practising witchcraft. Less well known are the persistent rumours of cults and covens within Grudge End throughout the eighteenth and nineteenth centuries, even during the height of the Industrial Revolution, when the area became more well known for its "dark Satanic mills" than for its involvement with demonology. It was not till the second half of the twentieth century, when most of the mills had closed or were closing, that public awareness of the true depths of devil-worship or witchcraft in the area became more widely known. Most of this was as a direct result of a series of horrific murders, most of which were, on the surface, unconnected, but all of which bore the tell-tale marks of demonism or sorcery. The worst of these were the murders of the Maguire family in 1983..."

Crompton's Guide to Demonology

"Kitty! Kitty! Kitt-eeee!"

Alice Briscombe padded out into the long, muddy stretch of her back garden with a plate of bacon rind, carefully placing her slippered feet on the flat stones that formed a meandering path of sorts towards the wooden gate at the end, where she could look out onto a back alleyway full of bin bags and other assorted refuse and the long brick wall of a factory, so tall it totally blocked out the sun till mid afternoon.

"Kitty! Kitty! Kitt-eeee!" she called out again. There was an answering chorus of meows, and three well-fed cats, a tortoiseshell, a large, fat ginger Tom and a sleek black and white, prowled quickly up the cobblestone alley between the heaps of garbage.

Alice had carefully cut the rind into small, manageable pieces, which she scattered in front of the cats as they swarmed in front of her for their morning treat.

"You shouldn't encourage those blasted strays."

It was a harsh, old man's voice, full of self righteous whinery, as she liked to call it, and Alice, retired herself, but a good ten years younger than old Mr Gaskin, turned with a shaking of her head to watch him struggle out of his back door, walking stick propping him up. His large, square head was brick red as usual – too much whisky the night before, she thought – which accounted for his grouchiness as well as his complexion.

"They're harmless enough," she told him. "And a lot cleaner than mice, which we might have far more of if it wasn't for them."

Mr Gaskin tutted disdainfully. "I've never had trouble with mice," he told her. "I keep a supply of poison for any of those blighters that are stupid enough to try setting up residence in my house. Perhaps I should spread some around for these blinking cats. They're more trouble than any mice, pissing and shitting all over the place."

"Now, there's no excuse for that kind of language," Alice rebuked him, though he'd always had a weakness for foul language whenever he felt out of sorts. "Or for those kinds of threats. If I find you've been poisoning any of these cats you'll have me to face, Mr Gaskin. And make no mistake: I'd make your life a misery."

"You make it a misery now, encouraging these mangy animals to flock around here. They were making such a racket the other night I could hardly sleep."

Must have been short of whisky that night, she thought, otherwise he'd have slept through a blitz.

Alice wandered back to her kitchen, where her husband, Harold, was sat at the table, nibbling on a slice of toast. A couple of years older than her, he hadn't been eating well for some months now, though he refused point blank to make an appointment at the doctor. "I'll be right enough when we've seen the back of this winter," he'd tell her whenever she got onto him about it. Today he looked even paler than usual, his lean face showing his years far more than it should. Even though it was almost twenty years since his nervous breakdown, the effects were still there.

"Not hungry?" she asked, his two slices of bacon untouched and even most of his fried egg still there on the plate, more messed with than eaten.

"This toast'll do me for now," he told her with a weak smile.

"Those cats eat more than you." She topped up his mug of tea, then poured one for herself.

"Have you been having words with Gaskin?" he asked.

"Silly old bugger was moaning about me feeding those cats again. Some folk get more miserable the older they are."

"Edgar was always a miserable tyke. It's no wonder his wife up and left him as soon as their little Sandra got herself wed. His wife was only waiting for the last of them to leave the nest before she bolted herself."

Alice Briscombe smiled at the memory. "Not that he didn't deserve it. I heard tell that he was a bit too handy with his fists in those days. I notice none of the kids come around to see him very often."

"Birthdays and Christmas – if he's lucky."

"Which is probably more lucky than he deserves."

"He's really got your gander up today," Harold told her.

Alice removed her bacon from the grill, then sat down to have her breakfast. "He was threatening to poison the cats this time."

"He's losing it, Alice. They'll be carting him off to a nursing home before long."

"And not before time, in my opinion."

Harold's smile grew broader. Alice had always been feisty. A trade union rep during her working life, she still did volunteer work on occasion. And found time to visit their allotment – which was something he only rarely had the energy for these days.

"Never mind," he said. "It'll soon be spring."

*

It was late afternoon, and what sun there was had risen far above the factory wall at the end of their terraced garden, filling it with a pale silvery light that, if far from spring, at least held a promise that spring was on its way. Harold was having a nap in the living room, the sound from the TV turned down so as not to disturb him, when Alice heard a sharp retort. She knew straight away that it had come from the back of the house, though she was not sure what it was. She did know the source of the screams of pain that followed it, though, in the alley.

She hurried out of the kitchen door and was at the backyard gate within seconds. Even so, the cat's cries had ceased by the time she got there, its chest still panting, though only just. Her face blanched as she saw the drops of blood on the side of its large, round, ginger head.

With some help from her husband a few minutes later Alice bundled the cat's body in an old blanket, then carefully laid it in a canvas bag that Harold used whenever he went fishing, which was rare enough these days. The Vets on Croasdale Road opened at 5.30, and she rang to make an appointment. Even though the cat was dead, Alice insisted on taking it to be examined.

"I want to know what killed him," she said. "And what caused that blood on the side of his poor old head."

It didn't take the vet more than a few seconds to inform them that the ginger had been killed by an airgun pellet.

"Fortunately the poor creature won't have suffered long," he told them. "Either a good shot or a lucky one. In any event it entered the brain. Would have killed it almost straight away." The vet scratched the back of his head. "I don't suppose you saw who did it?" he asked.

"I mightn't have seen whoever did it, but I do have my suspicions," Alice said, though her husband said she was

94

jumping to conclusions. "I can't see old Gaskin using an air rifle. It's as much as the man can do to stand on his own two feet with the help of a walking stick, never mind aim and fire a rifle."

"It could be kids, of course," the vet said. "There's always someone who thinks it's funny to take pot shots at cats. Dogs too, for that matter. Still, if you do see anyone with an air rifle it would be as well if you mentioned it to the police. They're hot on that kind of thing these days. It might be a cat this time, but it could easily be a child next."

That night Alice spent some time watching the gardens and alleyway from the back-bedroom window, but for all her vigilance she saw nothing suspicious. The next day she was careful to keep an eye on the two remaining cats when she'd fed them. But, fortunately for the cats, whoever shot poor old Ginger the day before, didn't have a go at either of the other two that day. Perhaps it wasn't Mr Gaskin, she thought, though the suspicion nagged at her and wouldn't quite disappear. He was cantankerous enough to have done it, but she did share her husband's doubts about his physical ability to aim and fire an air rifle in his state of health with any kind of accuracy. Poisoning the poor things was more his line of mischief, she thought – something which she hadn't forgotten about either. Just let him try that, she thought. Just let him try that and we'll see how far it gets him.

For the next few days things became peaceful once more and Alice fell back into her normal routine. She even managed to pass the time of day with Mr Gaskin in a reasonable pretence of neighbourliness, though she grumbled about it afterwards to her husband.

"Butter wouldn't melt in his mouth," she said.

"You still suspect him, don't you? For all that you've no real evidence against him."

"He would if he could," Alice insisted, though she knew as she said it that she was beginning to grasp at verbal straws to convince herself of the slim possibility of Gaskin's guilt. Which was really far from good enough. She imagined how she would have reacted to someone making unfounded accusations like that during her union rep days. No, she told herself. It was far from good enough. And, however much she knew she cared about and loved her wayward cats, she could not use old Gaskin's mulish dislike of them as reason enough to blame him for what happened to Ginger.

The next day Harold said that he thought he felt well enough to go to their allotment. It was a fine, bright day with an unseasonable feeling of warmth in the air. Alice was delighted, and prepared them a few sandwiches for while they were there, and a flask of coffee. It would take a good twenty minutes to get to the allotment and they would be ready for something to eat this afternoon.

Soon after she had fed the two cats, they set out.

The allotment was amongst about twenty others on several acres of land on the slopes above town, overlooking Grudge End, an area that had long since fallen into dereliction and was scheduled for redevelopment as soon as either the local council could afford it or a keen enough private company could be tempted into starting work demolishing the tumbledown streets of back-to-back terraced houses and closed-down mills.

Most of the allotments had belonged to mill workers on the terraced streets in Grudge End, but that was many years ago now. Most were rented out to people like the Briscombes, who made partially successful efforts at self sufficiency in growing vegetables and enjoyed the feel of rural life up on the heights, where the town petered out into moorland.

It was halfway through the morning by the time they walked there, after being dropped off by bus on the upper edge of the sprawling council estate that had been built alongside Grudge End in the late sixties, and from where most of the vandals who sometimes blighted the lives of the allotment owners came, though, thankfully, there had been a good long period of peace from that since the police stepped up their patrols around here last summer.

Even so, it was a shock to them both when the Briscombes

saw a tall young man in his early twenties moving about their allotment, a spade in one hand. He wore an old donkey jacket, with a long scarf round his neck like a student. His thick hair was partly held in place by a flat cap. He turned to face them as they approached the gate to the allotment.

"You are aware this is private property?" Alice asked severely.

The young man put down the spade. "I'm sorry if I startled you," he said. He had a pleasant, well modulated voice, and a narrow, almost scholarly face, with a trim nose, pale blue eyes and the wisp of a moustache about his upper lip. "I was just passing on my way to have a walk on the moors when I saw that someone had been trashing your allotment. All the canes had been trampled on and I could see footprints everywhere. I thought I would tidy up a little for you."

"And the spade?" Alice asked.

"I'm afraid someone broke into your tool shed. I don't know if there's anything missing, but some stuff, like this spade, had been scattered about. I thought I'd put it back for you in case it got ruined if it rains."

Alice opened the gate and peered about the long, rectangular length of their allotment. She could see straight away that the door to their shed had been partly wrenched off its hinges and now hung at an angle. As the young man had said, there were footprints everywhere, though the scattered canes had mostly been gathered in a neat pile.

"Thank you," Harold put in to help lighten the atmosphere. Though the young man was a stranger to them, there was something about him which seemed vaguely familiar to him. "That was kind of you. Most people would have just walked by." Which is exactly what Alice thought, as she wondered why he hadn't "just walked by" as well.

"Now you're here I might as well leave you to it," the young man said.

Alice would have said "Thank you very much," and let him go on his way, content that no more damage appeared to have been done than what she could see, but Harold said, "We're just about to have a bite to eat and some coffee. The least we could do is offer you a drink with us as a thank you for having tried to put things right. What do you say, Alice?" To which she could do nothing but agree, whatever her real feelings might have been. "Of course," she said, "though I'll have to see what cups are still left in the hut."

*

"What did you make of him?" Harold asked later that day when they had returned home and were sat in their living room, watching the 6 o'clock news on TV, warm in the glow from their gas fire, cups of tea at hand, and curtains comfortingly drawn against the night.

"He seemed amiable enough," Alice said, after a pause and some thought.

"You aren't entirely taken by him?" Harold suggested, uncertain why he felt as if Peter was someone he knew – or had known – which was ridiculous, considering his youth.

"I don't know that I am," she admitted. "I don't like to think ill of anyone – certainly not at first sight. But it does seem strange to me that he should have been so concerned at the little bit of vandalism that had been done there. It wasn't as if anything was even stolen – and we checked everything. And the only real damage was to the hinges of the hut and several canes. It was almost like pretend vandalism."

"Pretend vandalism?" Harold chuckled. "The things you come out with sometimes, Alice. Pretend vandalism!"

"You know very well what I mean," she scolded him. "If he hadn't been there we might have been a bit annoyed at the hut being broken open but we could have set everything right quick enough ourselves – and then forgotten all about it. Compared to what was going on last year this was nothing."

"Though it might be a warning of things to come," Harold added. "I think we should have a word with Ted Smith. As secretary for the Allotment Owners Association it's up to him to inform the police we might be heading for another problem with vandals. Wouldn't surprise me if police patrols haven't eased off since things got quieter there."

Alice agreed. "Though I still have my reservations about young Peter Hopkirk."

"At least we have his name. And where he lives. Randall Crescent."

"On the estate," Alice pointed out.

"But a part that's been mostly privatised. He said his parents bought the house when the council offered it to them."

"Hmm!"

Harold shook his head. "You take some convincing."

"I don't know," she said. "I just don't know."

*

Her doubts were hardly settled the following day when she went out to feed the cats and found Peter stood at their gate, a small bunch of flowers in one hand. Better than their spade, she thought to herself – but not much.

"A man at the allotments said where I'd find you," he explained as he offered Alice the flowers. "They're an apology for alarming you yesterday," he went on.

"I really don't know why. Your explanation was enough. After all, you aren't responsible for what someone else did up there. And you did try to put things right."

At that moment the two cats appeared, meowing for their treat.

Peter scooped the black and white one up in one hand.

"She's a beauty," he said. "Yours?"

"Only when she's being fed. Cats hardly belong to anyone," Alice said. "They're their own masters. Or mistresses, in Patch's case. They come here for their treats. Then they're off again." She watched him as he gently stroked the cat's chin while he held it to his chest. "You like cats?"

"Adore them," Peter answered. "We can't have any at home as my mother's allergic to them. But I'd have them as pets any time."

He did not overstay his welcome, though. Releasing Patch to get at its share of the bacon rind and the other titbits scattered on the ground, he said goodbye and strolled back down the alleyway.

As she turned to head back into the kitchen Alice caught sight of old Mr Gaskin staring out at her from his own kitchen, his large, florid face almost pressed against the window panes as he grimaced, pointing at the cats with a thick, stubby finger. It was on occasions like this that Alice wished their dividing walls were higher, even if that would have resulted in more shadows being cast in their back gardens. She frowned at him and hurried on her way. At least Peter, for all his unwanted attentions, did not share the irascible dislike for animals that her neighbour had.

*

During the following weeks Alice occasionally saw more of Peter. Often when she went out to get some shopping from the Spar on Croasdale Road or to visit the Post Office for their pensions, she would catch sight of him. Usually he only waved to her from a distance and that would be it. But, more often, as the days went by, he would be nearer and then he would ask her about her health and how Harold was doing and about the cats and if there had been any more trouble at the allotment from vandals.

Gradually, despite her initial doubts, she became used to seeing him about the area, so much so that she even began to cease wondering why he spent so much time wandering about the streets. She knew that he couldn't be a student as it was term time now. Of course, he might work nights somewhere, like Asda, she supposed, though she could not see him stacking shelves. Harold told her that she'd be surprised who ended up doing that these days, "the job situation being what it is." Still, whether he worked nights or not, he seemed to have plenty of time on his hands.

About a fortnight later, with the first hint of winter being on the wane, an event happened that changed things dramatically.

In actual fact it was two things, though they were only days apart. The first was when Patch failed to turn up with the tortoiseshell for its usual treat one drizzly morning in March. Alice was not particularly disturbed at this to start with. It was a vile day and perhaps Patch had decided to stay indoors wherever she lived rather than venture out in the rain. She had always struck Alice as a particularly fastidious cat, forever pausing to preen herself, and probably the prospect of getting thoroughly soaked in the non-stop drizzle outweighed the attraction of a few scraps of meat. But she also failed to turn up the following day too. And the one after that. By which stage Alice was beginning to get worried.

"Anything could have happened," Harold told her reassuringly. "Her owner might have moved house and taken her with them. That's usually what happens."

It was like him not to suggest anything worse, such as being run over by a car or any of the other accidents that could befall a cat that wandered about the streets and alleyways all day long.

On the fourth day, though, the tortoiseshell, Blakey (so named because his face always reminded her of the lanky inspector in *On the Buses*) was struck violently ill. He'd already eaten something in the alleyway before Alice got there. Instead of running to her as usual, the cat was struggling to be sick, its back heaving as it made a series of loud retching sounds. When these continued for more than a few minutes Alice became worried, especially when she noticed that there were several chunks of cooked meat, possibly beef, on the ground near the cat. She picked one up and put it in the pocket of her apron. There was little she could do for the cat as it continued to retch, so she went in to tell Harold what had happened.

"Do you want to take him to the vets?" he asked. "I'm sure

he'll see us straight away if the cat's as ill as all that."

Together they bundled Blakey up in the same old blanket they'd used to take Ginger in only a few weeks ago. Alice hoped, fleetingly, there wasn't an omen about this, before she dismissed the thought as foolishness.

The vet saw them almost as soon as they arrived and examined the cat thoroughly in his surgery. By now its retchings had ceased, but they seemed to have taken all the strength out of it, and it lay panting rapidly on its side. Alice handed the vet the chunk of meat she'd retrieved from the ground.

"I'll have this looked into," he promised. "It looks to me as if he's been poisoned. And with something particularly virulent, too."

"Not mouse poison?" Alice asked, remembering Mr Gaskin's threats against them.

The vet shook his head. "That takes much longer. It's an anti-coagulant, so the rodent bleeds to death, either through cuts and scratches or internally, and it can take several days. This is something much quicker." He glanced at the cat. "Leave him with me and I'll see what I can do. But I can't promise anything. It all depends on what kind of poison it is."

Later that day the vet phoned to tell them that Blakey was dead.

The certain death of two of the cats and the disappearance of the third left Alice feeling miserable. She had grown fond of all of them and looked forward to their daily visits, with their cheeky, welcoming meows.

"If that was that grumpy old neighbour of ours," she said to her husband, "I'll swing for him."

"Unless he admits to it we've no way of knowing," Harold told her, conciliatory as usual. "There are more people around who hate cats than just Edgar Gaskin."

The following day Alice bumped into Peter Hopkirk on her way to the Spar.

"What's wrong?" he asked immediately. "You look as if something terrible's happened."

When she had finished telling him about the cats his face had gone white.

"The evil old bastard," he said at last, so vehemently that Alice felt compelled to calm him down. "We have no proof it was Mr Gaskin," Alice said, wishing that Harold had felt fit enough to go with her to the shop. He was so much better than she was at being diplomatic. He wouldn't have let her even hint at the old man's involvement in what had happened to the cats – not without cast-iron proof.

"He's the only one you know of who's ever made any actual threats against them, though," Peter insisted, his lips thin with tension.

"That still doesn't mean he did it," Alice insisted. "Anyway, what's done is done. If it was him, let it lie on his conscience."

"If he has any," Peter added, bitterly.

That night, as the Briscombes lay in bed, Alice heard a muffled cry next door, then a series of loud bumps.

Alarmed, she nudged her husband awake.

"Something's happened at Mr Gaskin's," she told him. "I think he's fallen down the stairs."

"Drunk again, no doubt." Harold's voice sounded as if he was still half asleep. "I've heard him bumping around before."

"This wasn't just bumping around," Alice insisted. "This was worse."

Harold turned on the light. Alice almost regretted waking him: his face was pouchy with tiredness and more drawn than usual.

"Perhaps we should leave it till morning," Alice said. "We'll get scant thanks for disturbing him if he's drunk."

"We'd get scant thanks even if he's hurt himself," Harold told her. "But that doesn't mean we shouldn't find out. If you really think it sounded as if he fell downstairs I'll knock on his door and see what happens. I think I've a thick enough skin to deal with whatever he can come out with if he's all right."

Alice accompanied him as he got out of bed and slowly made his way downstairs. He put on his overcoat. "You wait here. I'll

103

only be a minute."

It was a blustery, cold night, and Alice regretted waking him after he set out, head bowed against the rain. When he got no response after three or four knocks he came back, dripping wet, and they phoned the police.

After that it was another hour and a half before they managed to get back to bed. A police car arrived within a quarter of an hour of their call and, after a quick discussion about what they'd heard, one of the policemen climbed over their backyard wall to see what he could make out inside Mr Gaskin's house. As the kitchen door was already open he went inside and found the old man's body tangled at the bottom of his stairs. Even though they radioed in for an ambulance, the officers confided that the old man was dead.

"Looks as if he broke his neck to me," one of the policemen told them. "And he did smell a lot of whisky, like you said he would. More than likely that's what led to him falling."

The next day Harold thought he might be starting with a cold.

"I should never have got you to go out in the rain last night," Alice said.

"You didn't get me to do anything," he rebuked her. "It was my choice to go and see if old Gaskin was all right, no one else's. You can't blame yourself for everything, Alice. Anyway, it'll pass in a day or so."

Later that morning Alice went out to get some medicine for him from the chemists. She had barely set foot on Croasdale Avenue when she saw Peter Hopkirk. He was stood in a shop doorway not a dozen feet from her, sheltering from the rain.

"Have you heard about Mr Gaskin?" she asked, stopping in front of him.

"Your neighbour? The one who hates cats?" Peter frowned. "What about him, Mrs Briscombe? Has he confessed to what he's been doing?"

"Hardly. He's dead. He fell down his stairs last night and broke his neck."

Peter whistled. "Can't say I'm all that saddened, Mrs Briscombe. Unchristian though that might be."

"I can't say that I am either," Alice confessed. "He was a foul tempered, vindictive man who drove most of his family against him, not to mention most of his neighbours too"

Peter smiled. "All's well that ends well, then, as they say."

"As they say."

By weekend Harold was on the mend and, with a sudden improvement in the weather, was keen to revisit the allotment. Neither of them had been there for several weeks now.

"If we don't do some planting soon it's going to be too late for anything this year," he said. It was also a way to relax after a visit by the police earlier that morning.

"You don't remember if you heard any other voices next door besides Mr Gaskin's?" they were asked by one of the same policemen who had answered their call earlier that week.

"I don't think so," Alice told him. "And Harold was asleep till I woke him, by which time everything was quiet again. Is there any reason we might have done?"

"We're not sure, Mrs Briscombe, but there is some evidence to suggest there could have been someone else in the house at the time."

"You don't mean it mightn't have been an accident?" she asked, but the policeman was non-committal. "That's not for me to say at this stage," he told her.

Which left them both feeling uneasy. There was the fact that Mr Gaskin's back door was open – an unlikely thing in their experience of their neighbour, who was a deadlock and bolts kind of man and the last person they knew to leave any outside door open at night, drunk or not.

"But you don't know," Harold said. "We all do daft things when we've had too much to drink."

It was half eleven by the time they reached their allotment and the sky was disappointingly starting to darken. As they looked downhill the derelict lines of terraced houses in Grudge End looked dismal and bleak, with an air of menace about the closed-down mills. It was a place Alice could never look at without thinking back to the 1980s when it was plagued by a horrifying series of murders, culminating in one entire household being slaughtered one night, hacked to death by one of its own members, who went on to take his own life afterwards, something which helped to hasten the district's decline. Harold had been an ambulance driver then and had been one of the first on the scene of the crime to take the bodies away. What he saw that day had so sickened him that he had suffered what today they called Post Traumatic Stress Disorder, but was then fobbed off as a nervous breakdown. Several months after the incident he had gone off on long term sick and never worked as an ambulanceman again. Not that the sight of the council estate to its left looked much better – nor any less menacing, with so many boarded-up windows along Shaw Crescent, one of its longest and most notorious stretches, a vicious haven for drug dealers and street gangs.

Things were not improved when they found their allotment had been vandalised again, as well as several others. This time it was not, as Alice had called it, "pretend vandalism". This was definitely the real thing. Their tool shed, where they sometimes sat on cold days and shared a flask of coffee in the warm shelter of its wooden walls, had been ripped apart, and it looked as if someone had even tried to pile some of its timbers into a bonfire. Of their tools there were only a couple of very old trowels and a rusted fork still left. Other allotments alongside had fared even worse, with greenhouse windows smashed in and young shoots ripped from the soil and thrown around like snowballs. There was even graffiti, "Dag woz ere" and "Fuck Off" prominent amongst them, sprayed everywhere.

The air of menace had suddenly shifted from the lower slopes to settle across the allotments, and both knew neither would feel like doing any work here today.

"Let's go home," Alice said. "It's getting colder again and it looks to me like it's going to rain later. We can get some fish and chips on the way and watch *Bargain Hunt* on telly to take our minds off everything."

It was a poor alternative, but one which appealed to them as they stood at the edge of the allotments, feeling isolated and under scrutiny on the open slopes above town, and the brooding expanse of derelict streets and the rundown council estate below.

They were only just in time to get some fish and chips when their bus dropped them off in town and they walked to the Happy Haddock on Bradshaw Street, near where they lived. As they left they saw Peter Hopkirk, stood in a shop doorway.

"Spends a lot of time doing that," Alice remarked, before beaming a smile as he waved to them and hurried over.

As usual he could tell that something was wrong, and as he walked with them to their house, he soon got the full story of the police visit earlier and what had happened to their allotment.

It was the latter that incensed him, though. "Those swine should be dealt with," Peter said, after Harold had invited him in for a cup of tea and a chip buttie. "The courts are too soft with vandals. And the police don't really try very hard to catch them either."

"It's difficult for the police," Harold pointed out. "They have other things to do besides keeping watch on our allotments. In any case they're easily spotted up there."

Peter nodded. "You're right, of course," he said.

"In a way I'm more concerned that someone else might have been next door when Mr Gaskin fell downstairs," Alice said. "The way the police were talking it sounded as if they wondered if he might've been pushed."

"Why should they think that?" Peter asked. "If he got as drunk as you say he did every night, he was bound to have an accident eventually. Especially when he wasn't all that steady on his feet to start with."

After Peter had gone they had another visit from the police. This time it was a plain clothes detective, D.C. Corrighan. He made himself comfortable in the spare armchair in their living room and smiled reassuringly as he explained that there had been a couple of curious finds in the old man's house next door.

"It was when someone noticed a complaint you'd lodged about a cat being shot by an air rifle pellet and another being poisoned recently. Air rifles and poison aren't normally things we expect to find in a house belonging to someone of Mr Gaskin's age – certainly not the kind of poison he had. Nor, for that matter, a powerful air rifle like the one we discovered in his bedroom."

Alice exchanged glances with her husband. For all that she had harboured suspicions about Mr Gaskin, it was still a shock to find out that it had been their neighbour all along who had done those terrible things to the cats.

"Rather disturbingly we also found a dead cat, smothered in a heavy-duty polythene bag. It looks as if it was deliberately trapped inside it, then suffocated when the bag was sealed with one of those plastic zip fasteners they use these days."

Alice felt herself grow faint, horrified beyond belief. That Mr Gaskin could have been capable of such wicked cruelty shocked her completely.

"I don't believe it," she murmured. Harold patted her reassuringly on her shoulder.

"We did find it a bit incredible ourselves," the policeman went on. "The dead cat was left on a table downstairs like some sort of trophy. We estimate it's probably been dead for a month or so now."

"I knew he hated the cats," Alice said, "but I never really thought he could have stooped to such wickedness."

"There is one curious thing," D.C. Corrighan added, watching them carefully with his doleful, deep brown eyes. "Because of some bruising on Mr Gaskin's shoulders, which look suspiciously like finger marks, there is the possibility that his fall might not have been accidental at all. As a result we've had his house checked for fingerprints. So far, though, we've not been able to find any that aren't Mr Gaskin's, which leads us to believe that he didn't get many visitors."

"Not even his family," Harold added. "Unless they had to."

"Mr Gaskin moved here from Grudge End, I believe," the

policeman went on.

Alice said that he had. "After his old house was condemned for demolition by the council," she said, "about fifteen years ago, before his wife left him."

"There are always odd things about some of the older people from that area. Some of the younger ones too, for that matter."

"It's always had a queer reputation," Harold said, his voice quiet, as unwanted memories of Grudge End came back to him.

"Killing and torturing animals was a recurrent problem there, from what I've heard tell at the station. So it looks as if Mr Gaskin might have brought that particular nasty habit with him when he came here. Leastways, that's how it looks to me. Not only that, but some of the books we found in there were not exactly your day to day reading matter either."

"Devil worship and stuff like that?" Alice asked.

The policeman nodded. "Well thumbed as well, which makes it look as if your neighbour had more than a passing interest. And might explain what happened to him in the end, if he was pushed down the stairs, as looks likely. You haven't seen anyone visit him lately? Any strangers, perhaps, in the area who may have had something to do with him?"

"He's always been a solitary type. I can't remember when I last saw him have a visitor," Alice said.

*

"Why didn't you mention Peter to him?" Harold asked after the policeman had gone.

"What do you mean?" Alice stopped in the doorway, on her way to the kitchen. "Why should he want to know about Peter?"

Harold frowned. "I'm not sure, but it struck me somehow that Peter could be involved."

"With what? With killing Mr Gaskin? With helping to kill the cats? You'll be saying next that he vandalised our allotment, for pity's sake. And I thought you always liked to be certain about your facts before you accused people of anything. You would have been quick enough to criticise me if I'd suggested something like that."

"I'm not suggesting anything," Harold protested. "I like Peter. He's forthright in his views. And honest. And caring."

"And yet you wonder why I didn't mention him to the police?" She shook her head, laughing. "Sometimes, Harold..."

Her husband laughed too, in response. "Perhaps we've just had too much of all this horribleness recently. We'll be a right pair of neurotic old biddies next if we're not careful."

*

Peter was stunned at the news about what had been found in Mr Gaskin's house. "It's just too bizarre," he said, as he shared breakfast with the Briscombes the following day. He had called round with the offer of going to the allotment to help repair some of the damage done by the vandals. It was only after he had eaten a plateful of scrambled eggs that Alice mentioned the policeman's visit the previous day.

"It was a shock to us both," Harold said. "Not least, the possibility that Mr Gaskin might have been murdered. Not something you expect to happen next door to you."

"It's unsettling," Alice added, though she felt that this was an understatement.

Peter sympathised. "I imagine it would be." His pale face was stern with concern. "I hope the police get hold of the culprit, if that's what happened. You never know where someone like that might strike next."

Alice felt a shiver of apprehension at the unwanted thought. "It is disturbing," she said. "Makes you feel unsafe in your own house."

Peter nodded emphatically. "Vandals on the allotments. Some sick pervert killing cats. Now the possibility that old Mr Gaskin might have been murdered. It's a nasty, vicious world we live in." Peter placed what was left of his last piece of toast back on the plate as a thought came to him. "You know, while

110

all this is going on, it might not be a bad idea if I stayed around here a bit more. As protection."

Alice laughed, though it was a forced, artificial laugh. "Do you honestly think we need some kind of protection?"

"You could have dismissed that idea for Mr Gaskin a week ago. And look at him now." Peter shook his head. "I don't know what's going on, but something is, for sure. And if someone really did push Mr Gaskin down the stairs it stands to reason it's not as safe as it seems anymore."

"But you couldn't possibly stay here all the time," Harold protested, disquieted at the thought. "What about your mother?"

"She's got my father. And my younger brothers are still at home, as well as my sister. Besides, she'd like to have more room in the house. She's always onto me about getting a place of my own."

"But you couldn't possibly stay here permanently," Harold said.

"I wouldn't need to. Just till whoever's been doing all this is caught. Or things quieten down. A couple of weeks, perhaps. That's all."

"I don't know," Harold said, uncertain. "I'll have to think about it. We both will," he added, glancing at Alice for support.

"I agree," Alice said. "We'd be asking too much of you. And unsettling all our lives needlessly."

Peter shook his head. "I hope it is needlessly. Anyway, the offer still stands If you change your minds I'm available. I just wouldn't want to see anything bad happen to either of you. I'd feel responsible if I didn't offer to help."

"That's appreciated, Peter," Harold said. "Believe me."

*

As the weather brightened during the rest of the week, the Briscombes decided to spend more time at the allotment. Ted Smith, secretary for the Allotment Owners Association, rang up

111

one night after tea to tell them that he had been in touch with the police, who had promised to step up patrols in the area and that things should improve. Though neither felt optimistic that this would be the end of the problems there, Harold said to Alice that they couldn't just leave their allotment as it was. "Besides which," he went on, "the fresh air will do both of us good." To which his wife agreed wholeheartedly. Ever since Mr Gaskin's death she had begun to feel claustrophobic in the house and welcomed the chance to spend some time in the open air.

They mentioned this to Peter, who said he would meet them there. He was still feeling excessively protective towards them and would have been upset if they had gone to the allotments without telling him.

Friday lunchtime they caught the bus to the edge of town and made their way through a blustery but dry wind to the allotment. Some of the damage done to the other allotments, especially the greenhouse windows, had already been repaired and much of the graffiti had been painted over.

"The place looks friendly again already," Alice said as they unlocked the gate into their patch of land and started to survey the task ahead.

"I wonder when Peter will turn up," Harold said. "I thought he might have been here already. He only has to walk up through the estate."

An hour went by as they pottered about the allotment, weeding and preparing the ground for some planting later on, and still no sign of Peter.

"You don't suppose something's happened to him, do you?" Alice said, during a break for some flasked coffee. She looked down the slope to the meandering avenues and crescents of the council estate, at the bottom edge of which was Randall Crescent and Peter's home. In contrast to neighbouring Grudge End, with its black slate roofs and semi-derelict streets, it looked bright, almost welcoming, if not for the reputation for vandalism, violence, drug dealers and crime in general. There used to be a joke that police patrol cars only ever drove through it in pairs.

Alice doubted if they ever drove through it at all these days in case they sparked off a riot. Though Grudge End, too, had its darker side, of course, as anyone who had lived here knew very well.

It was the following day that Harold decided to go out by himself. It was many months since he last felt well enough to do so, but the improving weather and the prospect of spring, made him feel up to it. Alice was far less sure and fussed over why he wanted to go out alone. For once, though, he was adamant. "It's not right that I can't do things by myself, that I tie you down to being with me all the time. If I don't try to get out and about by myself, I'll never get back into doing it again."

Alice understood. "Okay, but take care," she told him. "And don't do too much this time. I'll have a pot of tea waiting for you in an hour's time," she added.

Harold smiled, patted her on the shoulder, then zipped up his waterproof jacket and went out. It was cool but fresh today. Perfect weather for a bit of a walk. Work off some of the stiffness in his joints that spending too much time indoors had given him.

He had another reason, too, for wanting to go by himself. Peter's failure to appear yesterday bothered him. It bothered him more than he cared to let on to Alice. For all they knew Peter might be being questioned by the police. Harold still harboured vague suspicions about the young man's involvement with some of the things that had happened recently, though he had kept them to himself since the last time he argued about it with Alice.

It was only about half a mile to the edge of Peter's estate. Even so, Harold was beginning to feel the strain of walking by the time the opening to Randall Crescent appeared ahead of him. Peter had told them that he lived at number twenty-four. Harold's first sight of the house was far from promising, and he wondered just how honest Peter had been when he claimed his parents owned the house. None of those in the stretch facing him looked like they had been sold off privately, but bore the same lacklustre, neglected look of so many council-owned

113

houses on the estate. In fact, when he saw number twenty-four for the first time, it looked even worse than most of its neighbours. A short, weed-filled garden cluttered with bicycle parts, tyres, empty beer cans and an amazing number of broken toys, was the first thing he noticed when he stopped at the gate. Unfastening it, he picked his way along the concrete path, doing his best to void the dog droppings that littered it, till he reached the front door. There was a strong smell of burnt cabbage as he rapped on its thin, wooden panels.

Somewhere inside a child wailed. And a vicious-sounding dog began to bark, as scuffling sounds told him that the brute was struggling to poke its nose under the rotting wood at the bottom.

Inside he heard a man shout, followed by a thud, then a yelp, and the scuffling ceased.

A moment later the door was unlocked and opened. Despite himself Harold felt immediately intimidated by the tall, thin man who faced him. He wore a dirty grey t-shirt and baggy, food-stained jeans. In his early thirties, he had blood-shot eyes, at least three days growth of stubble on his scrawny jaws and a dull, aggressive expression on his face.

"I'm looking for Peter," Harold told him after a second's hesitation.

The man's eyes squinted at him as if he was uncertain what it was he was looking at.

"There's no Peters here, mate," the man rumbled.

"Peter Hopkirk? He said he lived here. With his parents."

The man stared at him as if he was slightly simple. "You takin' the piss?"

Harold frowned. "That's what he told me."

"Then he's a fuckin' liar. There's only me and the wife here and our son. And the tyke's only two. And he's not called fuckin' Peter."

Harold took a step back onto the path. "I don't suppose you know of a Peter Hopkirk anywhere round here? He told me he lived at number twenty-four Randall Crescent."

114

The man shook his head. "Never fuckin' heard of him." And with that he slammed the door shut.

Puzzled and disturbed by all this, Harold retraced his steps out of the estate and back to the main road. Why had Peter lied to them? He felt alarmed that both Alice and he had begun to trust the young man so much over recent weeks. If he hadn't come here today, they would have still believed what Peter told them about his family. Harold stopped. Up ahead of him, past a long row of shops and pedestrians, he saw a familiar figure. Or thought he did, as he wished his eyesight was sharper, certain it was Peter from the way he stood, with that thick mop of hair and the out of date look to his clothes. Peter was looking the other way and didn't appear to have seen him yet. On instinct, Harold stepped nearer the shop window alongside so he would stand out less if Peter turned around and looked in his direction.

In a way he was relieved that Peter appeared to be all right, but at the same time his unease was heightened. Why didn't he turn up yesterday like he said he would? And why the lies about where he lived?

As Peter set off up the road, glancing in shop windows, Harold decided to see where he was going. Perhaps he was heading home – his real home. He glanced at his watch, conscious that Alice expected him back within an hour. There were another twenty minutes to go. Though he didn't suppose it would matter if he was five or ten minutes late.

At the end of the next block, Peter turned off the main road up Duckworth Street, a short stretch that led under a railway viaduct to the start of Grudge End.

Fewer people ventured here. Fewer people had any reason to venture here. Virtually all of the houses were empty now and boarded up, awaiting the day when demolition would begin. Harold knew it would be more difficult in Grudge End to keep out of sight of Peter while he trailed him, though there were still some things that could provide cover. At this end some motorists used its streets for free parking while they went shopping in town or went to work, while some houses had thick timbers propped against their walls to prevent collapse.

Harold watched as Peter stepped into the gloom beneath the railway viaduct, his feet splashing through the deep puddles that were spread across most of the road, then headed up Grant Street. Harold quickly followed, walking as close to the walls as he could. Peter, though, never looked back once. Head low, he strode on as if with some purpose, and Harold was soon panting from the effort of trying to keep pace.

At the end of the third block, Peter turned right up a long, dark street that headed uphill at a steep gradient. Harold paused at the bottom, daunted. Tall, Victorian terraced houses faced him on either side atop elevated gardens, some with miserable-looking privets and stunted shrubs still growing in them. If Peter marched all the way to the end, at least five blocks further on, Harold doubted that he could follow him much beyond two. He knew he would be exhausted by then. He was out of practice walking these days and he could feel his heart pounding already. Despite the coldness of the day there was perspiration on his face and his breath was coming in gasps.

As he rested against the corner of the first house on the block he glanced up at the street name. He stared at it for some moments, unsure if he was reading it right, as the awful memories from over twenty years ago came flooding back. Randall Street. Had he and Alice misunderstood Peter when he told them where he lived? But who still lived here anyway? It was supposed to have been cleared months ago. A year, maybe. And Peter had clearly said that he lived on the estate, not Grudge End. They could hardly have mistaken that. But there was more to it than that. Randall Street was where the murders took place in 1983, the sight of which ended Harold's career as an ambulance driver. He could still remember those terrible nightmares that haunted him for years afterwards, of the sheer bloody carnage that he and his colleagues had had to deal with inside that house, where an entire family had been butchered to death, limbs hacked from their bodies and spread about every part of the house. These had been bad enough. The gallons upon gallons of blood that had soaked through every carpet and seeped through the floorboards and then through the ceilings to drip onto everything, that had been bad enough. But these weren't the worst. Far worse were the heads that had been hung by their hair from the banister rail, overlooking the stairs like a hideous line of trophies, their faces still showing the horror of what was happening to them. Their killer, the twenty-two-year-old son, had gone through his entire family in a murderous onslaught, first hacking at his parents' limbs to prevent them from being able to resist him, then working his way through his younger brothers and sister. Only then, as they lay dying from their appalling injuries, did he finish them off.

It was said at the time that Paul Maguire was obsessed with the occult. When found, he had sliced his forearms open vertically with long, deep gashes and bled to death, cross-legged within a blood-drawn pentacle in his bedroom. He'd pushed all his furniture to the walls and cleared the carpet back from the floorboards. Burnt-out candle stubs stood at every point of the pentacle, and the air within the curtained, gloomy room, was thick with the smell of hot wax and blood.

As the awful memories ran like a high-speed horror film through his mind. Harold wondered why Peter was coming here. He watched as Peter marched uphill, then turn and run up a short flight of steps to one of the houses. For a moment the young man stood there as he reached in his pocket for a key, then he stepped inside. Harold felt a tightness growing in his chest, as he hoped the house that Peter had gone into wasn't the one where it all happened, but he knew, even as he fervently wished it, that it would be the same. There was a certainty in him that would not be denied as he slowly, almost stumblingly began to climb the steep, flagstone pavement towards it.

Go home, he thought to himself. Forget it. Ignore it. Have nothing to do with it. Harold felt his legs weaken with fatigue as he trudged unwillingly up the street, till he was only two doors away from the house. *The* house. The house where the worst things he had ever seen in his life once lay. He looked up at its doorway. The door inside was open; within there was a dull twilight and he could just make out the damp-stained wallpaper in the vestibule. Its faded, floral patterning brought his memories back into even sharper relief. He would swear he could even smell the disgusting coppery stench of the blood that had drenched it. He remembered now for the first time in years the hearts that had been placed at every point of the madman's pentacle, the larger ones of his mother and father, and the smaller ones of his younger siblings. Five in all.

Harold felt tears well in his eyes as he reached for the granite gatepost and stared up the flagstone steps that led to the door. Every ounce of commonsense told him to turn away from it, but something stronger seemed to pull him towards it, despite the growing tightness in his chest or the ache in his legs or the dizzying shortness of his breath. He had to go in. He knew it. There was no choice about it. If someone had pointed a gun at him now and told him to stop, he would still have begun to climb those steps, then crossed the short path at the top to the door. There was a disgusting smell of damp and neglect and something worse. Something that still had the coppery tang of blood. His stomach muscles clenched as he breathed it in. But still he pressed onwards, his gloved hand extending to grasp the vestibule door and push it open. In times gone by there were local tales of witchcraft here in Grudge End. Three women were hanged in Lancaster, accused of sorcery in 1612. Those legends seemed to weave an atmosphere of superstitious horror about the place. Even though Sir Henry Malleson built his first mill here in 1848, and the long rows of terraced housing for his workers, none of this could wipe out the stigma of witchcraft and worse that still existed in this part of Edgebottom. A stigma that had come back with a vengeance as the mills closed down and people like Paul Maguire were drawn into the cults that had patiently persisted in Grudge End throughout those years. Even after the murders on Randall Street there were other incidents, Harold knew. Little wonder the local council were finding it difficult to find a developer to invest in this area as if fell into decay. Who would want to buy homes here?

Harold stiffened. As he slowly walked into the hallway, he heard footsteps deep inside the house.

"Peter," he called out. "Are you here? It's Harold. Harold Briscombe."

It had taken an effort of will to shout these few words, and the pounding of his heart was almost audible as he craned his neck to look up to the landing, from which years ago had hung those horrifying heads.

Harold narrowed his eyes to see through the gloom.

"Peter!"

The young man stood there, his face featureless in the darkness.

"I knew you would come."

"Peter?" Harold put one foot on the first step leading up to the landing. "Is that you?"

His face looked slightly different now. But it could have been the shadows, Harold thought. His damned eyes could cope with things so poorly these days.

Peter's voice was quiet in the echoing silence of the empty house. "The bait was just a tad too strong for you to resist, wasn't it?"

"What are you talking about?" Harold felt bewildered. He had intended to confront Peter with why he had lied about where he lived, but that didn't seem to matter any more. His presence here in this terrible old house was far more important. "Why here?"

Peter moved to the head of the stairs. "I feel stronger here. I was weak on the allotment, though that was once my parents', years and years ago, long before you and Alice ever even saw it." Peter smiled. "It was fitting to meet you there. After all those years. Though you seem no longer to welcome me. In fact, I sense you suspect me of being less than honest. Of having told you lies."

Harold felt tight bands press hard around his chest as he stared at Peter. His face, all those years ago now. His face...

"You were here," Harold said. His voice was hardly more than a whisper.

"I was not looking my best at the time," Peter said. His feet were almost soundless as he padded slowly, oh so slowly down the stairs, step by step. Harold saw his right hand move into the open. Saw the broad, steel blade of the large machete he was holding in his fist. Paul Maguire, he thought. His face and Maguire's. The more he stared up at him the more he looked the same. Even after all these years he could remember it again so well, though Maguire's face had been slack-jawed and sightless and drained of blood when he saw him all that time ago. He remembered, too, what happened that day when he reached to take hold of Paul Maguire's body to move him onto the body bag. The young man's blood-drenched hand had suddenly moved and clenched him tight about the wrist in what must have been a mindless spasm. The hand gripped hard, like a vice, and Harold remembered staring into the corpse's face as he struggled to pull himself free. In that instant, lasting only a few seconds, he saw the dead eyes stare into his, bare inches from him. He had gazed into them - into fathomless depths that made him feel as if he was perilously close to something agelessly evil, something so inhumanly cold and incalculably ancient. Then Nick, his assistant, reached down, prised the dead man's fingers from his wrist, and he fell back, free. Though the dark bruises, where he had been gripped, remained on his wrist for weeks afterwards.

Harold blinked, and the memory faded as he stared at Peter's face. A thin smile spread across the young man's lips. "You saw a little too much that day. Of the true me. Of the true spirit of Grudge End."

The machete rose, then fell. It sliced deep into Harold's shoulder. The old man had only enough time in which to cry out in shock as the blade cut through the thin material of his coat, parting his flesh with sickening ease, till it hit the bone. The pain sent waves of extreme pain through his body as he screamed out loud.

"First things first," Peter said. *"First things first."*

Though the sudden pain almost blocked every thought from his mind, Harold was aware of a change in the house around him. There was a feeling of life within it now. It seemed to rise from the old floorboards, up from deep beneath the earth. A deep, primordial hum of life, of things that were old when the Earth was young. Of the true spirit of Grudge End, which had altered and shaped those living here to its selfish ends. It was a spirit that was dark and powerful and so old that its age seemed to span dizzying depths of time.

Peter's face was rapturous with joy as he brought the machete down.

Again and again.

In sweeping, blood-stained, savage arcs.

Taking hand from wrist, arm from shoulder, foot from leg, and leg from trunk, before his final, merciless blow to the neck of the shuddering torso.

*

It was three months now since Harold set out on his walk and never returned. And though the police and the local media had spread an appeal for any sightings of him, no word had yet been received. Canals, quarries, reservoirs and pools had all been searched and sometimes dredged, but to no effect. It was as if Harold Briscombe had simply disappeared into thin air.

Peter had been as supportive of Alice as a friend could be. The couples' only daughter lived abroad. She had married years ago and she and her husband both had jobs and a growing family of their own in Australia. She came back briefly after Harold's disappearance, but she could not stay long, for all that she was as deeply upset as her mother. In the end, with many tears and promises to keep in touch and hopes for the best, she returned to her family in Perth. And Alice was left with her few old friends. And Peter.

Always Peter.

Peter the Rock, she sometimes liked to think of him.

She even began to share his growing interest in local history and the book he had started to write about Grudge End.

"Perhaps you would like to come with me as I explore it," he suggested one day in late August. "It's a fascinating place, for all that it has a grim history. I could show you some really interesting things I've come across there. Things that would truly amaze you."

THE WORST OF ALL POSSIBLE PLACES

1612

The minister looked around the tiny church. His followers were busy blockading the doors with everything they could put their hands on, from piles of books to the heavy, oaken pews, but he knew they were doomed. The Sheriff's men were already on their way from Lancaster, and it would not be long now before they could add their weight to the forces Sir Roger de Lacey had already mustered outside against them.

They would not get him to the gaol at Lancaster to be hanged for witchcraft, the minister thought as he climbed the rough wooden steps that took him to the top of the church tower. He looked out into the valley below where the small village of Edgebottom glowed with lights. Already there must be over a hundred down there.

The minister knew what he and his handful of followers had to do. This sacred site was theirs. Long before the church was built here there had been a shrine. No more fitting, welcoming place was there in the whole of Lancashire for them to die as true followers of the ancient gods. Their blood would be their final sacrifice.

He drew a dagger from his belt, then opened the sleeve of his shirt so that his lower arm was bare. When he returned to the floor of the church every eye was on him.

"Brothers and sisters," the minister called to them. "The time is upon us." With unhesitating speed he drew the blade of his dagger in a deep, straight line from his wrist upwards. Blood welled from the wound. And he watched with satisfaction as his supporters, heedless of the blows being battered on the doors, drew knives of their own.

*

Sticky heat played havoc with Bill Whitley's neck. Twice now he'd needed to probe a finger round the collar of his shirt, but to no avail, and he knew the real problem lay in the fact that it was just too tight. A couple of years ago it had fit perfectly. But too many beers and take-aways since his wife left him had added to his weight. Surreptitiously, he loosened the top button beneath his tie. The relief was immediate.

"Mr Jackson is ready to see you now," the receptionist announced. Bill wondered if there was a note of scorn in her voice, as if she had seen him fiddling around like a miscreant schoolboy waiting outside the headmaster's office.

Self-consciously, he felt at the knot on his tie, tightened it a little in a forlorn effort to smarten his appearance, then strode down the short corridor in the council offices to the door at the end. He knocked, then opened it.

"Come in. Come in."

Bill felt like saying "I already am," but didn't.

Wearing a suit that looked far too expensive to wear for work, Jackson, short, slim and giving off an air of self-satisfied complacency, was leant as far back as he could in the chair behind his desk. He watched while Bill, unavoidably prying a finger yet again beneath his collar, seated himself.

"I've studied your housing application as sympathetically as I can, Mr Whitley," Jackson said. "Unfortunately there is a severe housing shortage in Edgebottom at the moment. Last month alone we had to find places for over fifty asylum seekers."

Bill nodded. "Wasn't there something about that in *The Chronicle*?"

"Ah, *The Chronicle*." The corners of Jackson's pert mouth had a minute hint of scorn. "Their articles were not very helpful. More misinformation than fact, I'm afraid."

Bill nodded sympathetically. He had no idea what the man was talking about. Although he did remember glancing over the headlines, he had paid little more attention than that. Since his divorce he had had no real interest in newspapers, other than as something to shuffle in front of him while he worked his way through the first few pints of the night. Thinking of which made him wish he had decided to go along with his first inclination to have a whisky before his appointment at the housing office. It was too late now, but his fingers felt twitchy as the council official gazed at him.

"Things are getting desperate," Bill explained.

"You have somewhere to stay at the moment, though, haven't you?"

"A friend's putting me up on a bed settee in his living room. Not ideal. Tracey - that's his wife – she's had enough of me living there. It's three weeks now."

"Your own house was repossessed?"

Bill nodded.

"After I lost my job at the school I couldn't keep up the repayments. It was bad enough before my divorce, even with my ex's wage to help out. We'd gone into it way over our heads, especially when interest rates started to rise. From the start we began to fall behind on our repayments. After what happened, the court case and all, when I had to rely on unemployment benefit - "

"You have been trying for a new job, though?"

Again, Bill nodded, though the truth was he had made little effort. After he lost his job at St Cuthbert's Secondary School, he'd been unable to apply for any more teaching posts, and he didn't seem fitted for much else. Ten years as a teacher had seen to that.

"There aren't any council flats available at the moment that would suit someone of your background," Jackson said.

"What about flats that wouldn't suit someone of my background? I really am desperate. Another few days and I might be out on the street anyway."

Jackson stared for a moment at his fingernails. "There are *some* flats available, of course. There always are. In *certain* blocks. But you really wouldn't want one of these. They wouldn't suit you at all."

"Why's that?"

"For a start off you aren't a crack head, Mr Whitley. You haven't done time for armed robbery or mugging. Or selling drugs."

"It's only a roof and four walls I'm after. I don't care who my neighbours are. If it's only a matter of a few weeks - "

"Or months. Perhaps longer," Jackson said. "I can't guarantee how long it will be before we could offer you anything better. There are other people higher up the list. Single parent families, for instance. You're unmarried, a man and have no dependants. Unfortunately for you, that places you pretty low on the scale of priorities."

"A few weeks. A few months. I can survive that." Bill tried to put as much emphasis as he could on the sheer desperation of his need. It was difficult to express just how bad the situation at Wayne's was becoming. How could he explain the exasperation Tracey felt at his presence in their home, especially when he returned the worse for drink after a night out, drowning his sorrows?

"I don't think you fully appreciate just how bad some of these tower blocks are," Jackson said. "They're not safe. Some of the people living in them are on medication. They're schizophrenic - or worse. Some of them are downright dangerous. Quite honestly, I think a lot of them would be better off in a controlled environment than in the community. I wouldn't normally say this, but with your background it's plain to me how difficult you would find it living amongst them."

"But I wouldn't be living amongst them for long," Bill insisted. "Just *temporarily*. Till something better turns up. That's all, isn't it?"

Jackson shook his head. "You really don't understand."

"But I do," Bill said. "I appreciate what you are saying, but I need somewhere soon. A place of my own, if only for a few weeks. While I'm there I can keep my head down. Avoid the neighbours, if necessary. I don't care. When you've somewhere better, I'll take it. Gladly, I'm sure. Till then, I mean it, anywhere, *anywhere at all*, will do."

And, for all that he really still didn't appreciate just how sincere Jackson's advice to him was, Bill was satisfied that his

126

own assertions were justified. He could cope. He knew it. He was sure. After all, he'd managed to cope with all that had happened to him over the past twelve months. The court case for assault. The disgrace. His sacking. Having his face headlined on the front page of *The Chronicle*. "Teacher Found Guilty of Assaulting Pupil" – even though the boy concerned was a six-foot fifteen-year-old with a record for bullying other pupils. Even if Bill's mind had been obsessed with his own problems at the time and his head had been throbbing that day from a hangover a nearly full bottle of whisky had induced the night before – even if he had been more worried about his growing debts and his inability to keep up the repayments on his mortgage, or even remember half of the stuff he was supposed to be teaching that day, he could cope.

Jackson sighed. "I suppose it will be all right, so long as you know." He reluctantly picked up a sheet of paper. "There is a tenth floor flat we could offer you. It's in one of the tower blocks near Queen's Park Road. All of them are due for demolition next year, and all but one have already been emptied. One of them, Daisyfield House, is a sort of holding post, where anyone we've not been able to re-house elsewhere has been put for the time being. You could certainly stay there for the next few months. There's nothing in the way of furnishings. After the last tenant was removed – or left, I should say," he corrected himself, " – we had to fumigate the place. Some of them leave things in a disgusting condition. What furniture there was had to be destroyed, carpets and all."

"I've a few sticks of furniture of my own stored away," Bill said. "Enough for a flat."

"You wouldn't want anything too good," Jackson said. "Chances are it'd be stolen. Security's important where you'll be staying. Keep your door locked whenever you can. I don't want to alarm you, but the incidence of burglary in Daisyfield House is higher than anywhere else in Edgebottom."

"I'm a careful man," Bill said. "Belt and braces. I'll make sure the place is secure, even if I have to go out and buy some additional locks myself."

"Which wouldn't," Jackson added, "be as frivolous an idea as you might think."

*

"Thanks for your help, Wayne. I really appreciate it."

Bill stood by his friend's van, the back of which was loaded with most of his furniture – a bed, a couple of small armchairs, a table, a stool, a chest of drawers and a cardboard box filled with cutlery, pans, an electric kettle and a small TV, together with a couple of carrier bags of groceries he'd picked up from Asda.

The day had turned cold even for October, and the towering concrete blocks off Queen's Park Road loomed miserably before them against clouds that all but filled the sky. Set on the higher slopes of the broad, moorland valley within which Edgebottom had grown as a cotton town in the early decades of the Industrial Revolution, the winds here were notoriously fierce at the best of times.

"If I'd known how bloody cold it'd be I might have let you borrow the van and left you to come here on your own. I hope you've got some good heating up in that flat of yours. You'll need it." Wayne grimaced as a fresh gust swept over them. "Straight from Siberia, that," Wayne said, his teeth chattering.

"We'd better get on with it. The guy at the housing office said not to leave the van parked here too long."

"I know, I know. Otherwise one of those thieving bastards you've got as neighbours'll be away with it. Friggin' marvellous. I hope your ex realises what she's done to you."

"*I* don't," Bill said. "She'd be laughing her tits off if she could see any of this. Anyway, the sooner we start, the sooner we'll finish. Then I'll treat you to a pint or two at the Potter's."

The two men watched a pug-faced skinhead lurch from the direction of the flats, one hand stuffed in the pocket of his jeans. In the other he clenched a chain dog lead. An incredibly ugly pit bull terrier strained at the heels of his Doc Martins.

"Hey!" Wayne shouted. "Which of these is Daisyfield House?" From the ground they all looked equally derelict, with boarded up windows and entrance doors, as if they were all under siege, like some kind of modern-day Rourke's Drift.

The skinhead paused and looked their way.

"You looking for Daisyfield House, mate?"

"That's right. My friend here's moving in."

The skinhead laughed. "You must be fuckin' desperate."

Wayne sighed. Bill could see the exasperation in his friend's face. "That's right."

Laughing again, the skinhead jerked his head at the block to his left. "The door's a bit stiff, but if you give it a good push you'll get in."

The two men strolled down the slight incline from the car park to the entrance. Paint had been sprayed all over the boarded up windows on the ground floor and the doors into the lobby. Bill had to give the doors a hefty shove, using most of his weight, and it seemed for a moment as if they had been nailed shut, till they suddenly creaked and gave way beneath him. When his eyes adjusted to the gloominess inside he thought at first that the lobby was empty. Then he realised that a large, overweight man with dark yet somehow piercing eyes, was stood by the lift. Dressed in a baggy, dark blue suit, he looked over at the two men as they stepped inside.

"You new here today?" the man asked in a loud, pompous voice.

Bill nodded. "That's right."

The man smiled. "I'm the caretaker. I've been waiting for you, Mr..." He hesitated as he regarded Bill with a slight look of concentration. Bill disliked the way he stared at him, as if he was some sort of a seedy stage hypnotist. Perhaps even the caretaker in a place like this had to be a bit creepy, he thought. "Mr Whitley, is it?" the man said finally, a condescending smile on his long, lugubrious face.

"That's right. William Anthony Whitley. Bill to my friends."

The caretaker strode forwards. There was a key in his hand,

its palm the colour and texture of wet putty. "For your flat. Tenth floor. Number three."

*

Even after eight pints in the Potter's Wheel and a large glass of whisky when he eventually stumbled back to his flat in the early hours of the morning, Bill couldn't regard the sparsely furnished living room with anything other than a feeling of depression. Part of this could have been the dull forty-watt bulb he'd been provided with, which looked like cost-cutting gone mad to him, though he doubted he could spare the cash to buy a more powerful bulb in the near future. Besides, he reminded himself, this wasn't permanent. Only till the council had somewhere better for him. Or safer, he added. Outside on the corridor he could hear someone arguing. Only the occasional swear words rumbled through the walls with any kind of clarity.

Bill turned on the small TV he'd stood on a table by the central heating radiator, hoping to drown out the sound, then poured himself a second whisky. He had hardly taken a sip of it when someone began to pound on the wall from the flat next door. The thumps were so loud they could have been done with a hammer.

Shocked, Bill automatically turned down the volume on the TV. The thuds ceased at once, though he thought he heard someone laugh, then swear vindictively to themselves in a high-pitched voice.

Bill took a deep swallow of his whisky, glad that Wayne hadn't come back with him. His friend would have been banging on the wall by now if he'd been here. And swearing too. But Bill had soon begun to realise that even Wayne, whose aggressive tendencies rose to a peak each Sunday morning when he played for the Potter's Wheel Eleven, was out of his league here. The few other tenants of Daisyfield House he had seen while they were carrying his furniture to the lift had soon confirmed the warnings about this place that the housing officer had given him.

130

"Nutters and crack heads," was how Wayne had described them, when they'd eventually finished moving his stuff in and had driven off to the pub for a well-deserved pint. "No wonder the place is wrecked, especially that god-awful lift."

The lift had been more than an ordeal, reeking of urine and stale vomit, with violent graffiti daubed on every wall in various colours of felt tip pen and spray paints. "Probably used as a dog toilet," Wayne had suggested, after they had seen more tenants, in flagrant disregard of the council's no pets policy, taking short, squat, vicious-looking brutes either into the lift or off down the dark, concrete depths of the stairwell. "And what's that with all those friggin' pit bulls?" Wayne asked. "Is someone breeding the bloody things there?"

"Wouldn't surprise me," Bill said. "I don't suppose anyone from the council goes there to check."

"Not without a tactical armed squad from the police to back them up," Wayne retorted with a laugh that had a pitch of nervousness in it. "I'm bloody glad it's you, not me, that's moving into that shit hole, Bill. Makes me feel guilty seeing you move somewhere like that. Perhaps I should have a word with Tracey. I'm sure she'd understand if you came back for a while longer – at least till the council can fix you up with somewhere decent. If she took one look at that dump she'd agree."

Bill shook his head. "Honestly, Wayne, you've done more than enough already. I'll be all right. I'll only be there for a week or two. I can keep a low profile. Mind my own business."

"Put a chair behind your door. And watch your back," Wayne went on. He shivered melodramatically. "Anyway, mate, any problems – any problems at all – don't hesitate to call me. You know there's a bed settee available at a moment's notice if you need it."

As he sat in the dull silence of his flat at ten past one that night, Bill wondered whether he should have taken Wayne up on his offer.

*

131

The next day Bill woke up feeling cold and miserable. The central heating had gone off during the night and, despite fiddling with the controls for over an hour, he hadn't been able to start it again. Added to that, the large window in the living room rattled from the winds that wailed around the flats at these heights. An icy draft blew in from one edge of its metal frame, which he knew he would have to seal at some time, perhaps with tape.

Bill rubbed his hands together in an effort to generate some warmth, then bustled into the kitchen to prepare himself a mug of coffee. Asda's cheapest, Farm Store variety, since he couldn't afford anything better these days, topped with several drops of whisky to improve the taste. Cuddling the mug in his hands like a small, well-loved pet, Bill rambled aimlessly about his flat. As he looked morosely at the lack of comfort he decided that it could do with some rugs or at least some patches of carpet to cover the floor tiles, which were an ugly utilitarian grey, pockmarked with cigarette burns and dark, greasy, mouldy-looking stains. With only a few oddments of furniture, the place looked bleak, unloved and uncomfortable.

Dispirited, he topped up his coffee with some more whisky. The mixture seemed to be working well. And already he was beginning to feel less depressed than when he got up. Even the dark grey clouds that filled the sky for as far as he could see didn't seem quite so grim anymore. Tots of whisky and the minimal effort required in watching daytime TV were all that held him together most of the time these days. He would have gone for a walk, but the idea of using the lift was far from appealing, not with a hangover still playing havoc with his stomach, while the stairs were too much of an effort, even going down. Besides, the smell inside the stairwell was only marginally better than the lift. The drafts inside it helped to lessen the odours a little, but it would take more than those to clear them completely. Nor had he liked what he'd seen of the cack-handed drawings scrawled all over its concrete walls. Besides disturbingly graphic, crude depictions of copulation, there were other, even cruder scenes of violence, invariably splashed with daubs of red.

Having seen what some of the tenants of Daisyfield House had done to the place, Bill could understand why the council had decided to demolish these buildings. They didn't provide homes. They had become nothing more than gathering grounds for deviants, die-hard junkies and sick-minded psychopaths. And he was glad that he wouldn't have to live here for long.

Without warning, there was a sudden series of high-pitched, maniacal cackles next door. From the same flat, he realised, where someone had hammered against the wall last night. A few seconds later these were joined by low, bestial grunts.

Automatically, Bill reached for the whisky. He poured some into his empty mug. Gulping it down in one swallow, he wondered if he should hammer on the wall in retaliation, but he was far from certain how this might affect his neighbour. He didn't even know who lived there yet. Nor how many there were in that flat. What was it he had said to Wayne? Maintain a low profile? Keep his head down? And wait till the council could find somewhere better for him to live? Perhaps it would be better to stick to what he had said he would do. That would be the sensible thing to do. He drank some more whisky. But, as the cackling and grunts went on and on, with no sign of coming to an end, he began to feel angry. So angry, in fact, that, banging his mug on the table so hard he almost broke it, he stood up and, before he even realised what he was going to do next, he strode to the wall and slammed the edge of his fist as hard as he could against it. Twice, three times he hammered it again.

Almost instantly there was silence.

Amidst sudden qualms at what he had done, Bill unconsciously held his breath with expectation.

He did not have to wait long.

Retaliation came with a furious, almost insane storm of blows that shook the wall. Shocked at the deafening, ongoing onslaught, he stumbled away from it, appalled at the anger he could sense in the blows. They scared and alarmed him. It was as if whoever was doing it wanted to break through the breeze blocks and plaster to get in here at him.

Bill reached for the whisky and tipped what was left in his mouth.

On an impulse he put the emptied bottle down and scooped up his coat from the back of the armchair, where he'd slung it last night. His keys rattled in one of its pockets. After making sure that he had his wallet, Bill went and unlocked the door. When he stepped out onto the corridor he could still hear the bangs and crashes, though muffled now. Confident that whoever was doing it would be unable to hear his door being shut, he locked it behind him, then hurried towards the lift.

Several minutes later he was still waiting for it to arrive, with no indication that it was even working. He had heard that the lifts in these flats were notoriously unreliable. Perhaps it had broken down. If it had, there was only one other way out. He glanced towards the stairwell and flinched. Ten flights was a long way to go, and his legs felt wobbly after what he'd drunk. But there was no other choice, unless he went back to his flat.

With an irritable grunt, Bill started towards the stairwell. He tried to ignore the graffiti on its walls and the rancid smells that filled it with a doughy, almost palpable miasma. Here and there, someone had scrawled what looked like runic symbols amongst the obscenities. There was the occasional five-pointed star and, in one spot, in between floors, a detailed crucifixion had been painted in red and black. A hideously crestfallen Christ-like figure was nailed upside down amidst highly stylised flames. Though crudely drawn, with no pretension at art, it was nevertheless powerfully effective and, if he had been at all religious, Bill was sure it would have affected him more. As a piece of blasphemy it was even disturbing to a long-time agnostic like him.

By the time he reached the entrance hall, Bill was short of breath and beginning to feel dizzy as he trudged past the used hypodermics that littered the floor amidst dog-ends, dog-dirt and broken bottles. He could scarcely believe the local council was still housing people here. It was as if they had abandoned the place. No wonder Jackson had done his best to dissuade him from moving here. Perhaps he should have listened to him.

Outside, Bill stood for a moment in the fresh air, breathing it in, though even when he'd walked some distance down Queen's Park Road he could still smell the cloying, lavatory-like smells of the stairwell.

Like the tower blocks, most of the streets around here were due for demolition, with lines of poor, working-class terraced houses, and barely a garden in sight. Most of them dated back to Victorian times. Many were boarded up, derelict now, with gaps in their roofs where slates had either blown off or collapsed inside. Downhill there was a gradual improvement, with the occasional shop, while, near to the junction with the main road, Bill spotted a pub. He checked his watch. It was just past eleven. With any luck, he thought, the place would be open. More than ever the prospect of a pint of beer, a pie and some crisps and some sane company appealed to him. Smiling, he quickened his pace.

An hour later, three pints down, Bill was on his mobile to Wayne.

"I'd love to help you," Wayne said. "I really would."

"You did say that the bed settee was still available to me," Bill added.

"I did. I did. And I really, really wish I could tell you to pack your bags and come around now, but Tracey's mother arrived today. She'll be with us for at least a week. You understand, don't you? I'd help if I could." Wayne took a deep breath, obviously embarrassed. "You've not even been there a full day yet. Surely it can't be that bad? I know it's not good, but how bad can it be?"

How could he explain it? Bill stared round the pub. It was so comfortable in here – plain and simple, homely even – that it was difficult to get his head round just how repulsive Daisyfield House was. How disturbed he felt there. Especially when he hadn't even met his neighbours yet. Even telling Wayne about the banging on his wall or the high-pitched laughter didn't seem credibly unnerving.

"Look," Wayne said, "we'll get together tonight. Have a few pints. Tracey won't mind. Give her a chance to have a natter with her mum. Gives me a chance to get out of the old bat's way. What do you say?"

Bill agreed straight away. After they had made their arrangements, he rang off and reached for his beer, though he knew he would have to take it easy if he was going to have a session with Wayne tonight. He'd have one more pint, perhaps buy another meat and potato pie, then amble up the hill to Daisyfield House.

And hope that someone had got the lift working by the time he got back.

Whether it was the alcohol or tiredness, but the walk back several minutes later seemed longer and harder than it should have been. The day had grown gloomy and a mist was beginning to close in on the heights at the end of Queen's Park Road. By the time he reached the rundown streets which immediately surrounded the tower blocks, the mist had solidified into a dense fog. The temperature had dropped and Bill shivered beneath his coat as he hurried the last few yards to his own block of flats. He didn't like his obscured vision. Odd shapes seemed to loom through the fog. Figures which lurched onto the edge of his sight, then veered off again and disappeared before he could get a clear impression of them. Almost as if they were playing games with him. He pushed open the door into the flats, then pressed for the lift. To his relief the indicator light came on at the top. A few seconds later the steel doors opened.

A short man, stocky, with deep set eyes beneath a thick, woollen hat, was stood at the back of the lift, leant against the wall. His denim clothes looked old, careworn and grubby. From around the soles of his tatty-looking Nike trainers a dark puddle was starting to spread across the floor of the lift. Bill stared at it for a moment in disbelief, then looked again at the man's face. His expressionless, grey, almost vacuous face. There was no reaction in it. No movement. And at first Bill was puzzled. Was the man drunk, high on drugs or seriously ill? For a moment more Bill stared at him, waiting to see if he would make some effort to leave the lift. Instead he remained motionless, apart from the widening pool about his feet. Uncertain, Bill wondered whether to step into the lift, ignore the puddle of what he was sure was the man's urine, and press for the tenth floor. But there was something about his face that worried Bill. It was too still. Too pale.

As if he was dead.

No sooner had Bill thought this than the man began to shudder, pushed himself up off the wall, then staggered forwards. He stared at Bill, dull eyes vacuous like those of a drunk, before he pushed himself past to walk, stiff-legged, out of the lift.

*

"I'm not exaggerating," Bill said, later that night in the Potter's Wheel. They'd had a few rounds by now and Bill was not bothered any more how foolish he sounded.

For his part, Wayne had begun to accept much of what his friend said to him with an open mind.

"It's a piss hole," Wayne said. "And that fellow just went on to prove it." He put down his half emptied pint of beer. The Potter's Wheel was busy tonight with a darts match between the home team and one from the Bell and Compasses, and he had to raise his voice to be heard. His face became serious for a moment. "You are taking care to keep a low profile, aren't you?"

"Of course I am," Bill said, "apart from banging on the wall when that idiot next door started to cackle like a maniac."

"Be careful, Bill. Some of those guys would be better off in an asylum. The rest aren't that much better. You remember that murder a year ago? The girl who killed her boyfriend with a friggin' chainsaw while he was asleep in bed? That was in those flats."

"Wasn't she an out and out pot head? Off her head on drugs?"

"Which doesn't make it any less real. For all you know you might even be in the same flat. There was another block there that was even worse. They shut that one down after some idiot cult got a grip on a group of people living in it. Ended with some kind of mass suicide. A dozen or so of the mad fuckers, from what my wife told me before I came out. She remembers shit like that, God bless her. Not like you and me, who've only got time for the sports pages."

Bill drank some more of his beer, thought about what Wayne had said, then shook his head. "The only problem I have is that nutter next door. *Eek eek eek,*" he imitated badly. "I know some of them are dangerous. Which is why I want to get out of there as soon as I can."

"And why I feel guilty about not being able to put you up till you can get somewhere better," Wayne admitted

Bill shrugged. "It's my fault. I should have listened to that guy at the housing office. He tried to warn me." He gazed at his beer for a moment, lost in thought. "You know, that bugger in the lift really put the wind up me. I watched him go across the lobby towards the doors. The way he walked you'd have sworn he was an extra from a George Romero zombie flick. If I'd been anywhere else I'd have cracked up laughing. As it was, I couldn't wait for the lift doors to shut."

"Even with his piss all over the floor?"

Bill shook his head. "If it was piss," he said. "It didn't look all that much like piss really. Not when I looked at it. Of course, there was no way I could tell from the smell. It stinks like a friggin' toilet anyway."

"Too fucking true," Wayne added.

"And I can't say I was particularly keen on looking too closely at the stuff. Though I had to keep my eye on it. I didn't want any of it touching my shoes."

"What makes you think it wasn't piss?"

"It didn't look right, somehow. Too dark. Though that could

138

have been the dirty floor."

"Perhaps something got spilt in the lift and your yobbo friend stepped into it, too doped up to notice."

"Though it was still spreading while he was stood in it. And I'd swear some of it had dribbled down the legs of his jeans."

Wayne shook his head. "I don't know what to say. Perhaps you should see if you can get the council to re-house you somewhere else. Tell them you've been threatened."

But Bill was unsure. "That might get the police involved. I don't fancy that." Not after his conviction last year. There were too many unresolved grudges amongst some of the police who'd been involved, especially after his suspended sentence.

When they left the Potter's Wheel an hour or so later, Wayne's taxi dropped Bill off at the end of Queen's Park Road. As the car sped off, leaving a wake of mist in the frosty air, Bill stared for a moment at the imposing bulk of the tower block ahead of him. Few lights showed in any of its windows, and it loomed like a huge, black monolith. Even one of the supposedly empty blocks had more lights on than Daisyfield House, making it look, by contrast, even grimmer.

Bill hurried the last few yards to the lift. This time, though, there was no response when he pressed the button. Bill felt his stomach sink as he realised that he would have to climb the ten flights of stairs to his flat

In desperation he went to the caretaker's office, but the door was locked and no one answered his knocks. Not that he really expected anyone to be here at this time of night. Finally convinced that he had no other choice, Bill trudged towards the stairwell. His legs felt heavy. And he knew that the amount he'd drunk in the Potter's Wheel had not prepared him for a climb like this.

Despite this, though, he managed to make it past the first two floors without too much trouble. Head down, eyes fixed on the steps ahead of him, he even avoided having to look at most of the drawings and other graffiti that covered the walls. By the third flight, though, his gasps were starting to hurt his chest. Too many fags and too much beer, he thought to himself between wincing at the pains that razored his ribcage. Hauling himself, one step at a time, he grasped on tight to the banister rail for leverage.

After five flights, though, he had to rest. He couldn't go any further till he'd caught his breath. A half flight more and he was sure he would have a heart attack.

Wheezing badly, Bill let himself slump onto the concrete steps. He no longer cared how filthy they were, though he could feel their icy coldness strike through his clothes and deep into his buttocks.

Fewer of the wall lights were working here and the place was sometimes so gloomy he could barely see the stairs ahead of him. Then he would come to an area that was so brilliantly lit that, however much he tried to resist looking at them, the graffiti would almost leap out at him from the walls. Bill stared at the agonised expressions on their crudely drawn faces. Someone up here was seriously disturbed. At this level there were other figures too, large and lumpy, round-headed shapes with obscure faces. These, somehow, were even more repulsive than the rest.

As he rested, slumped against the steps, Bill heard something move on the floor above. It sounded as if someone was dragging a heavy sack.

With a grunt of effort, Bill forced himself to his feet. He knew he couldn't rest for long or his muscles would start to stiffen up. They were aching already.

Eight steps later and, finally, he reached the next floor. He glanced at the closed doors into the corridor to his left. Through the wire-mesh and glass security panels, he could see someone halfway along it, bent almost double. Perhaps that was who he'd heard, he thought. Bill squinted through the panel, with its odd distortions, puzzled and beginning to feel concerned at what he could make out. Perhaps the figure wasn't moving at all, only one of its arms? As he approached the glass for a clearer view, his breath caught in his throat. He stopped, took an involuntary step back from the doors, glad they were shut, then narrowed his eyes. He was certain he'd glimpsed what looked like a knife in the figure's hand. It was long. And pointed. A kitchen knife. The kind he would have used for carving a joint.

He heard the knife strike whatever it was hitting with a meaty *chunk*.

Trembling, Bill hurried back to the stairs. Even with a stitch that almost doubled him up he managed to climb the next three floors before he was forced to stop once more. When he did, he almost collapsed on the steps in a sodden heap. Sweat stung his eyes, and he had to reach into his trouser pocket for a handkerchief to mop them with. If he had been cold before, he was roasting now. And exhausted. He stared through the gloom at the floor he'd just left, trying to control his breathing so that he could hear if there was anyone there. *If anyone had begun to follow him.* But nothing moved. Even though he could still make out the faint *chunk-chunk, chunk-chunk* from far away. Steady. Relentless. Machine-like. On and on and on.

Bill gulped. Again he forced himself to climb the stairs.

Only a few seconds later the stabbings stopped.

Or perhaps he'd climbed too far to hear them now?

Bill paused. He held his breath, certain he could hear something move. As if the doors onto one of the corridors below were being opened.

And someone was coming out of them.

Panicking, Bill pushed himself towards the next bend on the stairs where he wouldn't be visible from the floor below. Though why he felt the almost desperate need to conceal himself from whoever was down there, he wasn't sure. Irrational, he knew. But he couldn't ignore his gut instincts. And, despite his exhaustion, despite the red-hot pains in his chest, he forced himself to keep on going, till his feet were clear of the next bend in the stairs.

Only then did he stop.

Only then did he wonder how far he had to go till he reached his flat. By now he had lost count of how many flights of stairs he'd climbed. Was it nine or ten? Or even more? Had he passed his level?

Bill stumbled towards the doors onto the corridor. It looked like his, and he wondered if he could have finally made it. He fumbled in his pockets for the key to his flat. Already he could hear footsteps echoing up the stairwell. The outer doors swung shut behind him as he started to run towards his flat. Only then did he see one of the apartment doors ahead of him open. Light leapt across the corridor as a man looked round the doorway at him, perhaps disturbed by the sound of his feet. He was short and skinny, in an oversized combat jacket and jeans. His mouth opened wide in what looked like a protest, then Bill pushed him into the room.

"No!" the man managed to squawk as he tumbled over the tattered wreck of a settee behind him. "Get out of here!"

But Bill could already hear the doors at the end of the corridor open. He pushed the apartment door shut behind him and fastened its locks. Only when his back was pressed against it, did he look at the man he'd forced into the room.

"You can't barge in like this." The man's scrawny face was contorted with indignation and fear. His voice was a pathetic whine. Thin strands of hair hung over his face, though much of his scalp showed through on the crown of his head, pink and shiny.

Bill glanced around the flat. Apart from the settee, which looked like it had been salvaged from a refuse tip, with stains and tears on its old-fashioned covers, there was no other furniture in the room. It was more like a squat than a rented flat. There weren't even any blinds or curtains at the window. Take-away cartons littered the floor amongst scattered bottles: White Lightning, sherry and non-generic bottles of vodka. All of them empty. On the seat of the settee Bill noticed an old tin box. Beside it lay a dessert spoon, heat-stained and grimy, with some kind of dark residue on it, and a heavy-looking hypodermic.

An alcoholic junkie, Bill thought to himself in disgust.

The man giggled in fear as Bill stared at him. Hearing the high-pitched sounds, Bill suddenly realised who he was.

"You banged on my wall," Bill said, unable to hide his disbelief.

"*What?*"

How often had he heard that self-righteous whine from horrible little brats at school? "Last night. When I turned on my TV. You banged on my wall, you fucking bastard. And again this morning."

As he looked at the man's perplexed eyes, Bill wondered whether he even remembered doing it.

Before Bill could say anymore, there was a loud scratching at the door behind him. The little man stifled a yelp, then crouched, cringing, behind the settee.

Bill turned and saw the door handle move. But the two locks, a solid Yale and a heavy bolt with a security chain attached to it, held firm. As he watched the door, Bill felt himself start to share his neighbour's fear. His throat felt dry and he could feel his bowels melt inside him. He'd be shitting himself in another few minutes, Bill realised, though he felt no humour at the idea. He moved away from the door as the furious scratching started again, so hard he could see the panels shake.

"What the hell is it?" Bill asked.

The little man shushed him to silence. His face trembled with agitation.

"*It'll hear,*" he whispered tensely.

It seemed as if whoever was outside the flat had heard him, though, as the scratching paused, then started again even more fiercely than before, as if an enormous rodent was trying to claw its way through.

"What the fucking hell is it?" Bill asked.

"*Don't!* It'll know we're here."

"It knows we're here anyway," Bill said. "Whatever *it* is."

"*Not so loud!*" The little man held his hands up for emphasis, and Bill was surprised to see how violently he was shaking. "Move away from the door. *Please!*" In his agitation, he almost dragged Bill back across the room to the window.

"What do you know about whoever's out there?" Bill asked.

"Haven't you heard it? Night after night. Walking up and down the corridors."

"I've only been here since yesterday. I didn't see anything when I came back last night."

"You used the lift?"

Bill frowned. "It was working then."

"Not now?"

Bill shook his head. "I had to come up the stairs."

"Despite those warnings?"

"What warnings?"

"On the walls? Those warnings painted on the walls?"

"That bloody graffiti?"

The little man laughed contemptuously. It was laughter, though, that was edged with fear. "You were lucky, mate. Others haven't been. I heard one poor sod earlier tonight. Must've been new here, like you. Probably thought it was fuckin' squatters' paradise. Till he found out different."

"I'm not a squatter," Bill said.

The little man scoffed. "You're not telling me the council sent you here? If they did, they'd have sent you to Daisyfield House."

"What do you mean? This is Daisyfield House."

"Like bollocks it is. That's the one nearer the road. This fuckin' shit-hole's been condemned for months. No one lives here now except those of us who've broken in. That's why there's no maintenance on the lift. Now and then it works. But that's sheer luck. Surprised there's still any power. Shouldn't be, by rights." He peered at Bill. "You telling me you thought this dump was Daisyfield House?"

Bill remembered the skinhead who'd directed him here. *The door's a bit stiff, but if you give it a good push you'll get in.*

"That's rubbish," Bill said finally. "I was given my key by the caretaker."

"The caretaker? What fuckin' caretaker? There's not been a caretaker here since they decided to close the place down after what happened last year."

"There was one when I arrived," Bill insisted. "A tall man. Long faced. With piercing eyes. He had a rather nasty pallor."

The junkie shook his head.

"Someone's been having you on. They shut this place down after all those deaths."

"What deaths?"

"It was a suicide cult. Twelve of them topped themselves. Even their leader, some mad arse called Chambers. It was in all the papers."

Not for the first time, Bill regretted his inability to pay any real attention to the news these days. "It may well have been," he said, uncertainly. "If it was, I didn't read it. Anyway, you've got to be mistaken."

"If I am, it'd be a surprise to those of us who are squatting here."

"And what kind of people are they?" Bill asked.

"There aren't so many of us. It's only 'cause we've nowhere else to go. And we're careful. Keep ourselves to ourselves."

"Like hammering on my wall last night?" Bill said.

"That stuff will have made me," the little man said. He pointed at the syringe on the settee. "I go off my head sometimes."

Bill thought he was probably a bit "off his head" most of the time. He'd even managed to spook him over whoever was scratching at the door. Though Bill had to admit he had frightened himself in the stairwell even before he got here. Whoever was out there was probably just another drugged-up squatter. Though not necessarily harmless, he thought.

"Are you staying here all night?" the little man asked. He squirmed inside his oversized combat jacket like a skinny kid playing at soldiers in his father's clothes.

Bill hadn't thought about staying here, though he didn't feel like opening the door just yet. Whoever was out there was still clawing at it. Nor had he forgotten the knife he glimpsed earlier. If it was the same person he saw on that corridor, the only option he had was to wait till they'd gone. Either that, he thought, or phone the police. Bill reached in his pocket for his mobile phone. "Damn it," he grunted. The bloody thing had no signal...

"You can use the settee if you like."

Bill looked at it. The stained fabric was so filthy he would have been happier on the floor, except that the shag pile carpet looked even dirtier.

With what he'd drunk and the strain of climbing ten flights of stairs to get here, Bill was feeling exhausted already. Perhaps a few minutes rest would help to revive him? Shaking his head, he let himself slump on the settee, surprised that it was much more comfortable than it looked.

And, although he hardly trusted the junkie, Bill felt sure that if the little man did try anything stupid, he could handle him. He knew that part of this feeling of complacency was because of all the alcohol he'd drunk, that if he was sober he'd probably not take his eyes off the man. As it was he felt far too tired. Even with the non-stop scratching at the door, he began to relax, and it was all he could do to keep his eyes open.

Some time later - it could have been hours; it could have been a scant few minutes - he awoke with a jolt. Everything was in darkness, except for a thin beam of moonlight. He felt cold and stiff and he grunted with the effort to move his cramped-up legs. His mouth tasted of stale beer.

And for a moment he wondered where he was.

Then he started to recall what had happened since his return to the flats.

Alarmed by the disjointed memories that came back to him, Bill stared around the twilit room. There was silence now. Whoever had been scratching at the door had gone. And Bill grimaced as his memories of the evening became even clearer. Where was the junkie who lived here? Groaning, he pushed himself to his feet. Though there wasn't much light, there was enough to make things out, even the tin box and the hypodermic that had been abandoned near the window, monochromed by the moonlight.

Then he saw where the little man had fallen asleep on the

floor, knees drawn up towards his chest. He was very still.

Disturbed, Bill stepped towards him, aware that the junkie's chest didn't seem to be moving. Cautiously, he knelt beside him, his knee caps popping with twinges of pain, and gently tried to wake him. The shoulder beneath the damp material of his combat jacket felt unnaturally thin. And Bill felt nauseous touching it.

"Hey!" he whispered, as loudly as he dared. "Wake up!"

He pushed him again. This time harder. And the man's body, which was even lighter than it looked, began to roll over. Gasping for breath at the sudden shock of what he was looking at, Bill saw there was barely any flesh beneath the pale grey skin on the junkie's face. It was stretched and wrinkled and damp with mould. Dark holes stared at him from where the eyes should have been. With a hand to his mouth to stifle the almost automatic urge to vomit, Bill realised in horror that the man he was looking at must have been dead for months.

Who the hell, then, did he speak to earlier?

Repulsed and frightened, Bill stepped away from the body. He stared at the baggy combat jacket and the dirty, patched-up pair of jeans, through which the hard outlines of the man's skeletal legs could be clearly made out. He knew these clothes were exactly like those worn by the junkie. He even recognised the thin strands of hair hung over the ruined face. Everything about him, his size, his clothes, his hair, even the shape of his almost non-existent chin, was exactly the same. But how? Bill could not understand what he was looking at. It was insane. *Madness*. It just did not make sense. Unless he was starting to hallucinate. Perhaps too much alcohol. Or too much stress. Or the trauma of living in this place. But he knew he was desperately trying to rationalise things in an effort to make sense out of what had happened. What else could he do? Accept everything that appeared to have happened as reality? Accept that he had spoken to a man who'd been dead for God-knows how many months? Whose face was no more than skin and bones, whose only colour were the layers of mould that were growing on what was left of him?

For the first time in months Bill felt the shakes in his arms and legs. It had been so long a time since he'd had them last that he really thought he'd been cured. Now, more than ever, he felt convinced he'd been teetering on the edge of another breakdown for some time. Which was why he knew he should never have come to this place. It had been a mistake. He couldn't take it. Stumbling into the junkie's apartment and finding what was left of the man's body must have been enough to push him over the brink, that and all the alcohol he'd been poisoning himself with for the past few months.

Hands quivering, Bill reached inside his jacket for his mobile. He would have to let the police know what he'd found. He didn't dare do otherwise. He knew his fingerprints would be all over the flat. As these were already on record, if there was anything suspicious about the man's death, he didn't want the police to think he had had anything to do with it, even if the man had been dead long before he got here. But there was still no signal on his phone. Either the walls were too thick or there was something wrong with the nearest mast. Frustrated, Bill put it away. He'd have to try and ring them later. He could have tried going back downstairs to see if he could get a signal outside, but there was no way he was going to do that yet. He was too exhausted. And too fuckin' frazzled, he thought to himself with a desperate attempt at some sort of humour.

He unlocked the door to the corridor. It was time to get away from this flat and return to his own. God, he thought, he'd even had hallucinations that this wasn't Daisyfield House at all – as if he could place any credibility on what he thought he'd been told by someone who was already dead! Bill grimaced as he glanced at the body near the window. Later, when he'd had some sleep, he'd phone the police and let them know what he'd found, though he winced when he thought about all the inevitable questions they would badger him with. He would also make an appointment with his doctor. Perhaps he could prescribe some pills for him that would sort him out. Maybe even help get him out of this hell hole and somewhere safe. Somewhere where his mind could cure itself.

Though what he felt most in need of now was a glass of whisky.

He could almost feel it on his tongue already, burning away the aftertaste of last night's beers. Steadying his nerves.

Bill looked both ways down the corridor, then stepped out of the junkie's apartment. With less than a third of its lights still burning, the corridor was worryingly gloomy, with far too many shadows along it. They made him feel uneasy as he remembered some of the things his memories told him had happened earlier that night. Things which he was certain must have been his own imagination.

As he approached his apartment Bill wondered what time it was. His watch was useless. Its battery had run out weeks ago and he'd forgotten to replace it. Outside it was still so dark it could have been the middle of the night. Apart from the moon, everything was black. When he'd glanced out of the junkie's window he'd been unable to see a single street lamp, as if everything below was covered in fog.

A few strides took him to his door. He looked forward to tumbling into bed and a few hours sleep. Time in which to try to forget about the body next door – and all the other self-induced terrors he'd been frightening himself with tonight.

He'd hardly started to turn the key when he heard someone scream.

It was a woman's scream.

Full of fear.

And loathing.

And desperation.

No, no, no, no, NO, he thought. And for a moment he hesitated, key in hand, ready to ignore it. He'd had enough already. He was whacked. Exhausted. Ready for nothing more than to close his eyes and try to forget all the nightmares his over-exhausted mind had been frightening him with.

The woman screamed again, hysterically now, and he knew

that he would have to do something, even if it was only to see what was going on.

Reluctantly, Bill pocketed his key and stumbled back towards the stairwell.

Now, more than ever, he felt the need for a glass of whisky. Sweat soaked his skin. It felt hot and rancid beneath his clothes, and he was sure he must stink.

At the doors into the stairwell he paused for a moment to catch his breath and steel his nerves. Then he pushed the doors open.

The screams were even clearer now.

"Hey!" Bill shouted in what he knew was a pathetic effort to scare whoever was making the woman scream. His voice cracked with tension. "What's going on?"

Grumbling to himself, Bill started to clatter down the stairs, making as much noise as he could. He was not a brave man, and he knew it was probably only a residue of the alcohol he'd drunk and remnants of adrenalin from all that had happened that were making him act even now. *That and not knowing what was down there, he thought.*

A memory flashed back of a half-seen figure with a knife in one hand.

Chunk-chunk! Chunk-chunk!

And Bill hoped to God that *that* was something his drink addled mind had dreamt up for him. It hardly seemed credible he could have seen something like that even here.

Two floors down and the screaming suddenly stopped.

In the abrupt silence Bill's mouth felt dry. His heart pounded. And his hands began to shake once more.

"Bugger," he muttered to himself, sotto voce.

He had two choices now. Either turn back and try to forget what he'd heard or keep on going and see what was there? Bill dithered. His conscience told him that he had to keep going, that someone might need his help. On the other hand, whoever had made the woman scream might still be down there. He had seen enough of the kind of people who lived in this place not to wish to pit himself against them.

Bill took a few more steps down the stairs. Slowly, reluctantly, he approached the next bend, more alert than he'd been in years. His whole concentration was so focused on listening for sounds of movement or a glimpse of someone down the stairs that he was barely aware of the graffiti on the walls.

Hardly daring to breathe in case he made too much noise, Bill turned the next bend.

The pool of blood on the landing below was so large that at first Bill did not realise what it was. Uncomprehending, confused, he stared down at it. It almost filled the entire floor between the doors to the next row of apartments and the stairs. It had already spilled over the topmost step.

When he finally realised what it was, Bill threw himself back from the sight and gagged with nausea. He turned away from it, and for a moment he thought it had to be another hallucination, that there really wasn't anything there at all.

But when he looked again nothing had changed. Almost black in the twilight, the blood looked fresh. And there was so much of it. Pints upon pints of it. More than he had ever seen in his life.

His breath rasped through his chest in ragged gasps as he began to retreat up the stairs. He knew he had to call the police. Perhaps if he climbed to one of the higher levels he would get a signal on his mobile. Down here there was nothing more he could do – except risk meeting up with whoever had caused this bloodbath.

Before he had taken more than a couple of steps, the doors onto the corridor below began to open.

A shadow fell across the landing. Alarmed, Bill turned and began to retrace his steps up the stairs as fast as he could.

The shadow was large and lumpy.

And barely human.

One hand raised above its head, the shadowy fingers looked long and thin. In Bill's heightened nervousness they seemed far too long - and far too thin.

And even though he knew that the shadow could have been wildly distorted by the angle of the light behind it, he was too unnerved to wait and see any more.

Bill had only just turned the first bend in the stairs, his heart pounding hard enough to have alarmed him earlier with thoughts of coronaries, when he heard someone step onto the landing. He could hear their breathing: *their heavy, raucous, asthmatic breathing.*

At last he looked back.

An old man, a kitchen knife shakily clasped in a liver-spotted hand, was stood on the landing. There was so much fear on the old man's face that Bill immediately knew there was no threat in him, despite the knife. Dressed in a scruffy old woollen jumper and brown pants, he wore a shapeless pair of well-worn slippers, all of which added to his look of harmlessness.

The old man stared at Bill with glistening, pale pink eyes. Apparently unnoticed, the pool of blood almost touched the toes of his slippers.

"What's going on here?" The question came in a tremulous whisper.

And Bill wondered what an old man like this was doing here. If the housing office had serious doubts about sending Bill to this place, how many more doubts should there have been at letting a man in his seventies or eighties end up here? It didn't make any sense. For God's sake, he thought, this was a dumping ground for junkies and psychos and social dropouts, not feeble old geriatrics.

"I don't know what's been going on," Bill said. "I was going to try and get a signal on my mobile higher up the stairs. To call the police."

"Mobile?"

Hearing incomprehension in the old man's voice, Bill rummaged in his pocket for his four-year-old Nokia, though the man's face showed no more understanding even when he saw it.

"Mind that blood," Bill warned as the old man started to shuffle towards him for a clearer view of the phone, and for the first time appeared to see the blood on the landing. His response was a strangled grunt of horror. He stumbled backwards, at the same time waving the kitchen knife in front of him as if in some way that could ward the blood away from him.

Alarmed that the old man was going to hurt himself, Bill hurried down the stairs, circled the edge of the blood, and took hold of the man's free arm. He'd no sooner touched him, though, than the old man flung his other arm round. Bill saw the knife blade flash, reflecting light from the neon strips above, as it darted towards him. There was a burst of pain as the knife cut through his sleeve, and Bill realised, with a feeling of shock, that he had been stabbed. Instinctively, he lashed out. His fist glanced off the old man's face. Then, reeling and dizzy from the pain in his arm, Bill snatched at the knife, wrenched it sideways, and felt it come free from the old man's grip.

"You fucking old bastard," Bill complained in disgust. Holding the knife in one hand, he started to back away from him, then turned and splashed and skidded across the blood towards the stairs.

Even as he grabbed at the banister rail for support, he sensed movement behind him. Something hard and sharp bounced off his shoulders. He squawked in surprise, tugged at the banister to get away from whatever had hit him, and started once more to climb the stairs. But whoever was behind him had not given up. And again something heavy crashed onto his shoulders. This time it caught. And Bill gasped at the pain as he wrenched himself free. Ready, though, he had the kitchen knife gripped in his fist. Bill glimpsed something tall and dark move behind him and jabbed out at it. The knife jarred as it hit something that gave beneath its sharpened point.

He saw the old man's face, distorted in pain, too close to his own.

Taller now, more menacing, with hands that reached towards him with splayed, long-nailed, nicotine-stained fingers, the old man grimaced with effort. Bill gasped, then stabbed him again. The knife hit hard into the old man's jumper. Sank deep

153

into it. Blood instantly soaked its bobbled fibres.

Shocked at what he had done, Bill saw the old man clutch his chest, then collapse on his knees. The liverish wattles on his neck quivered as he looked up. His rheumy, almost blind-looking eyes were consumed with hatred as he stared at Bill. For a moment more he grasped at the knife wounds. Blood bubbled from his mouth, before he fell onto the landing.

Even as the old man hit the ground, Bill raced up the stairs, unable to believe that he had been forced to stab him. He stared in horror at the blood on the knife blade. With his criminal record, he knew he could never convince the police he'd had to do it. It was as if he was in a nightmare, in which events piled up on top of each other, each one worse than the last. How many times had he stabbed the man? Twice? Three times? More? He knew the police would never believe it was self defence. If he had stabbed him once, maybe. But twice? *Three times?*

Bill knew he would have to get rid of the knife and any of his clothes that had the old man's blood on them. Anything that could link him to what had happened.

By the time he reached his own floor his eyes were burning with tears. He could barely breathe, and what breaths he took came in torturous wheezes. He knew he had reached the end of his tether. Physically and emotionally he couldn't take much more. All he could think of now was to get back to his room, where he would strip off his clothes, bundle them up with the knife, then take a long, hot shower to wash away every vestige of blood off his body. Come daylight he would go downstairs, get rid of anything that could incriminate him, and hope that that would be enough, that he could convince the police, if they came to ask him any questions, that he had had nothing to do with it.

As he approached his flat, Bill saw that the door to his neighbour's room was open, though he was sure he'd shut it behind him when he left.

Cautiously, he hid the knife in his coat pocket, then slowly moved towards the doorway. He could hear music.

Bill looked into his neighbour's apartment and was relieved

to see that it still had the appearance of a squat, though now there was a small CD player on the windowsill; green lights oscillated across its display screen in tune to the music. Outside the large, curtainless window the night looked just as dark as before. The junkie, whose body Bill last remembered as a desiccated corpse, curled like a grotesque foetus beneath the window, sat cross-legged and breathing shallow, trance-like breaths near the CD player, while he stared across the room with vacant, drug-dazed eyes. His mouth hung loose, a dribble of saliva caught mid-drip on his glistening chin.

Relieved, but bewildered that the man wasn't dead, that he must have imagined the months old corpse, Bill hurried past before the junkie noticed him, then reached for his keys and let himself into his flat, certain now he was suffering from some sort of a nervous breakdown.

He wondered, sickly, just how much of what had happened was real.

Bill laid the knife on the kitchen table, its blade still slick with blood. Had he really used it to stab the old man? *If* there had ever been an old man. *If* he hadn't just been in his imagination or part of some crazy nightmare.

Unable to trust whatever he remembered anymore, Bill wondered if this was what it was like when someone began to lose their mind. He stared at his face in the mirror above the sink. In his reflection he looked old and haggard, with eyes that were desperate, blood-shot and full of fear. Sweat sheened his skin, which was grey and lifeless in the stark neon light.

Though it probably looked grey and lifeless in any light now, he thought to himself.

Bill opened a cabinet next to the sink, took out a bottle of whisky and poured himself a large measure in a plastic mug. He emptied it urgently, in a gulp that left his throat feeling raw.

He'd needed that.

He'd really, *really* needed that.

Though he knew he would need much more than this before he could rest.

155

Resignedly, his head beginning to ache already, he refilled the mug.

At some time during the next few hours he somehow managed to fall asleep. There was no more than an ashen hint of dawn through his living room window when he awoke, feeling stiff and sick. A migraine pulsed inside his head with agonising intensity. Hardly willing to open his eyes again, he rolled over on the settee he'd fallen asleep on, as disjointed memories from the night before came back to him.

There was a buzzing sound. It was this that had woken him, penetrating his sleep like a bad toothache.

Feeling fragile, every joint in his arms and legs aching so much he wanted to cry out at the pain, Bill placed his feet on the cold surface of the floor.

It was then that he realised that the buzzing sound was his doorbell.

Bill groaned. Who the hell could that be?

His mouth dehydrated like a sun-dried sponge, he pushed himself off the sofa and walked, stiff-legged, to the door. He peered through the spyhole.

The distorted image of Wayne's face stared back at him through the fisheye lens. There was someone beside him, but Bill could only see part of a shoulder.

A woman's shoulder.

"My God, you look wrecked."

"Thanks, Wayne." Bill cast his friend a poor pretence at a smile as he stepped back, letting him in.

"I hope you don't mind that I've brought Tracey," Wayne said. "I thought she ought to see this place for herself - to see how bad it really is."

Bill waved them in. "Forgive the mess. I haven't had time to tidy up yet," he joked feebly, his head aching so much he found it hard to concentrate on what he was saying.

"Wayne told me how awful it was. But I didn't realise just how bloody awful till we got here," Tracey said sympathetically; her presence somehow helped to brighten up the room.

Bill glanced at them both. "Did you use the lift?"

"Too true we did. Can you see Tracey trailing up those stairs? All ten flights?" Wayne laughed, though Bill could see the concern in his eyes. "Been on the sauce already?" Wayne asked.

"What else is there in this bloody place?"

"I think I would have been tempted to join you," Tracey said with a broad, sympathetic smile. Which was a miracle for Tracey, who normally had an annoyingly puritanical attitude towards drink.

"Why did you decide to come so early?" Bill asked.

"Early?" Wayne glanced at his watch. "It's nearly noon. That's hardly early, even for a man of leisure like you."

Bill looked at his window. What hints of light he could make out through it were so dull it could have still been night. Wayne followed his look and expressed surprise.

"How dirty are those bloody windows of yours?"

"Hardly dirty at all," Bill mumbled. He crossed the room, opened the door onto the small, concrete balcony. Even outside it was dark. What light there was didn't come from the sun but from a sliver of moon high in an otherwise pitch-black sky. When he looked down to where he should have been able to observe Queens Park Road there was nothing but darkness. Like before, no street lights showed, as if there had been a power cut.

"What kind of a crazy, fucked up place is this?" Wayne asked.

Bill shuddered. "I don't think you and Tracey should have come here."

"Don't be ridiculous," Tracey said, but Bill could hear doubt in her voice, as she stared through the window, her brows furrowed with a look of perplexity. "There must be a heavy fog or something."

"There was no sign of fog when we got here," Wayne said. "Everything was clear."

"Then it must have closed in while we were in the lift."

Wayne snorted, though he too had begun to look worried. "You must be joking. We were only in it a few minutes. That

157

wouldn't have been long enough."

"It must have been," Tracey insisted. "It's here now, isn't it?"

Wayne shrugged. "Of course it is."

Bill watched them argue with feelings of unreality. They too were being caught up in the shear oddity of this place. Its lack of rules. Its bizarreness. Its bloody ridiculous lack of credibility.

"Hey," he interjected. "There's probably a completely logical explanation." Even as he said it the words sounded ridiculous. There was nothing logical about anything he remembered happening here since he arrived.

Bill returned to his living room.

"You should leave. Both of you," he said. "We all should."

"That's what I came here for," Wayne said. "That's why I brought Tracey. So she could see." He stopped, as if he realised just how much he had underestimated this place. He looked at Bill for help.

"I need some water," Tracey said suddenly, her face pale. "This is getting too much." She headed for the kitchen. Even as she moved Bill suddenly remembered the knife he'd left near the sink, but before he could forestall her Tracey had already gone. Her cry of disgust was immediate. "Wayne!"

Bill's friend glanced at him, almost reproachfully, as if to say "What the bloody hell have you done now?" - then followed his wife into the kitchen. His own response was just as blunt. *"Fuck!"*

Wayne stepped back into the living room, the knife held between his thumb and forefinger with a look of disgust. It looked even worse than Bill remembered. Most of the blood had dried into ugly, red-brown crusts. Even the hilt was caked with it.

"What the hell was this thing used for?" Wayne asked, accusingly.

Bill shook his head. "I don't know. I'm not sure." Which he knew was the truth.

"It looks to me like something you shouldn't have been able to forget," Wayne said.

Tracey appeared beside him, white faced and looking sick. "I think we should go."

Wayne looked again at the knife, then flung it to the floor.

"I don't know what's been going on here, Bill, but you need to sort yourself out. Unless things have already gone too far."

"What do you mean?"

Wayne shook his head. "I think you might know." He nudged the blood-caked knife with the toe of his trainers. "Where the hell has all this blood come from, Bill?"

"You wouldn't believe me. I don't even know if I believe what I remember happening here last night myself."

"Are you being serious or are you simply going off your head?" He looked as if he would have added "again" but had held back from doing so.

"Probably I am going off my head," Bill admitted.

"Perhaps we should get going now," Tracey suggested to her husband.

"You'll come with us?" Wayne asked. He was watching Bill doubtfully.

Bill nodded. "I hate this place. I don't ever want to come here again."

He could tell, looking at Tracey, that she was unsure if she wanted him to go with them or not. But what could she say? Stay in this dump while we desert you? Bill tried to smile reassuringly at her, but his face felt as if it was stuck in some bizarre sort of rictus.

It was then that Bill's sometimes dead, sometimes spaced-out junkie neighbour decided to burst out in a series of high pitched, maniacal giggles that came through the wall as if it was no thicker than a sheet of paper.

Bill saw Tracey jump with alarm. Instinctively, she moved closer to her husband, who put an arm protectively over her shoulders.

Bill shrugged. "Par for the course in this sodding place."

Wayne grimaced. "I'll take your word for it, Bill."

But Bill's attempts at levity hardly mirrored his own anxiety.

He could feel a subtle change in the atmosphere. Though far from warm earlier, the air felt icily cold. It had a chill that penetrated deep inside him. And he half expected to see the air before their faces mist whenever any of them spoke. With a suppressed shudder, Bill headed for the door. At the last second he felt an intense premonition of dread, even though he knew it was really no safer inside his flat. Whatever madness had taken a grip on this place was no weaker here, he was sure. With an instant's hesitation, he pulled the door open, perhaps harder than he had intentioned. The lights along the corridor flickered, as if ready to expire. Shadows juddered back and forth, especially at the far end, where the lights were weakest.

"Someone should have paid the electricity bill," Wayne muttered as he followed Bill. Hugging herself against the cold, Tracey stepped out close behind him.

As soon as he'd shut the door they headed towards the lift. Again Bill saw the door to his neighbour's apartment was open. Light from inside spilled out onto the corridor. The little man's ridiculous giggling sounded even louder now. And Bill hesitated at passing it, worried what he might see inside – and even more worried at how his neighbour would react if he saw them. But there were three of them now, and their numbers gave Bill a vague feeling of confidence. He looked at Wayne, whose frown seemed even darker now, then continued forwards.

Whatever he might have expected to see when he looked into his neighbour's flat, Bill was totally unprepared for the hunched-up, grey-faced creature crouched, open mouthed, beneath the dark window, giggling insanely. The junkie's face looked barely human. And Bill was sure, no matter how many drugs the man was on, that these could not account for the grotesque contortions on his face. His mouth was open far too wide for anyone whose jawbone hadn't been dislocated. Nor could drugs account for the jagged lines of teeth exposed between his lips like shards of broken pottery. While his outspread fingers looked impossibly long. And made Bill shudder as he recalled the claw-like hands that reached out for him last night.

160

Tracey could not restrain a squeal of fear when she looked in the room. The junkie's eyes peeled away from whatever dreams he had been gazing at to focus on her, red-rimmed and oily, with a look of decay.

Acting on instinct, Bill lunged into the room, grasped the door handle and, as the little man started to lurch forwards like some strange, ungainly beast, slammed the door in his face. There was a violent thud, then an infuriated scrabbling as sharp fingernails scratched at its panels.

"Keep going," Bill said. His voice was hoarse with tension. The scratching on the thin, wooden panels reminded him of those that had scared him last night. Which did nothing to lessen his feelings of dread, especially when he remembered talking to the man only hours ago.

Must get out of here, Bill thought to himself. I must. *I must.*

Wayne jabbed at the button by the lift. But the indicator light above the door refused to respond and, even though it might have been working perfectly well a few minutes earlier when his friends got here, Bill knew the lift wouldn't come for them now.

"It's useless," he said. "We'll have to use the stairs."

Tracey stared towards the stairwell with a look of disgust. Even here they could smell it. And to Bill it seemed much worse than he remembered. Something new had been added to its usual odour of stale urine. A sour, coppery kind of smell. Like blood, he realised, as he remembered the massive pool he saw last night only a few floors below. He had begun to hope that that had been part of some bizarre hallucination, a drink-induced madness that didn't exist outside his mind. Unless, he realised, all of what was happening now was a part of that madness. That he was trapped inside it.

He felt sick and empty at the thought.

"We've no choice, have we? We'll have to use those fucking stairs," Wayne said. "Come on, love," he added to his wife. He gave her a reassuring hug, then headed for the stairwell. Bill wanted to warn them to take care, but Wayne was in too much of a hurry, taking the stairs two steps at a time. Tracey struggled

161

to keep pace in her high-heeled boots and had to grasp the banister rail for support.

Bill trailed increasingly further behind them. His legs were still too stiff to attempt to keep up with his friends. Nor did he have the stamina now. It was not long before their footfalls began to fade into the distance as they disappeared into the depths of the building. And once more Bill felt as if he was alone in this place.

When Tracey screamed a few minutes later, he was not surprised. He had been dreading and fearing and expecting it. This place had far from finished with them yet. It would take more than a headlong dash down the stairs to get out of here.

Almost at once he heard Wayne shout something in anger, but even with all the floors in between Bill could hear the fear in it too.

"God, no," Bill mumbled. He tried to run faster, though he knew that whatever was happening he would be too late to do anything about it.

Tracey screamed out again. This time Bill was certain it was the scream he had heard last night. Its pitch, its fear, its disgust, its horror were unmistakeable.

Deja *fucking* vu, he thought, trembling with fear. He didn't want to go down there. He knew that he couldn't stop whatever was happening to his friends. That all he could do was get himself killed as well.

Or worse.

Trembling, he stood in the stairwell, unable to make himself go any further. Next to him on the dirty concrete wall was the blasphemous painting of the upside-down crucifixion he saw last night, with its stylised flames. A Christ dragged down into the depths of Hell. A fitting touch of spay-painted artwork for this place.

Impotent with fear, Bill could only listen to Tracey's screams and Wayne's increasingly more frantic shouts. Tears in his eyes, he gazed desperately along the wall to where there was another painting. This showed a bizarre version of the Last Supper, surrounded by a circle of ugly, squat-bodied dogs. All of the people in it wore modern day clothes. And each had huge, vertical cuts the length of their forearms, as if they had sliced themselves open to commit suicide. Blood spurted across an oblong banquet table. At the head of it, his arms cut like the rest, was the thirteenth figure, standing in a mimicry of Christ. His long, pale, staring face looked so much like that of the caretaker. He remembered what he'd been told about a suicide cult that established itself in one of these blocks. A cult that ended in a dozen deaths. Was this someone's crude depiction of what happened there? And had the caretaker somehow been involved in it?

A sound further up the stairs made him spin round in alarm.

The junkie was stood, looking down at him from the next bend in the stairs. The little man's face had reverted back to a semblance of normality. He looked concerned. And frightened.

"Go down there and he'll get you," he said in not much more than a whisper.

"Who will?"

"You know who. He runs this building."

"Chambers?" That was the name, Bill remembered now. The cultist who'd persuaded those others who had joined his group to end their lives.

The junkie snickered nervously. "Don't say it too loud. He'll hear you."

"Will you help save my friends?" Bill asked.

"And get both of us killed?"

Bill felt tempted to tell him he was almost certainly dead already, even if he didn't realise it. He remembered the desiccated face he'd seen in the junkie's flat last night, the little man's skeletal shell of a body curled up on the floor like a badly preserved Egyptian mummy.

"What would you suggest we did?" Bill asked. "I don't want to stay here."

"Do you think you have a choice anymore? It's *his* place now. *He* decides who goes or stays."

163

"But why? And how?"

The little man merely shook his head.

"I'm going back to my rooms. It's safer there." He paused as the screams and shouts from down the stairwell suddenly ceased. "There's not much time. You can come back with me. Or stay and face whatever's down there on your own."

Bill glanced into the gloom below. He felt sick at the silence. He felt sicker still when he realised that the silence was far from absolute. That he could hear something being dragged. And the *chunk-chunk, chunk-chunk* of a knife being stabbed into meat. Slowly, mechanically, on and on …

But it was the sound of footsteps coming up the stairs that jerked Bill into making a decision.

Hastily, he followed the junkie up the next few flights of stairs, the aches in his legs all but forgotten in his urgency to get away from whatever he could hear below.

As soon as they arrived back at the little man's flat, the junkie quickly locked the door, then offered Bill a seat on the sofa before going over to start rummaging furiously through some old newspapers scattered by the kitchen door. He brought one over. It was a tattered, year old copy of *The Edgebottom Evening Chronicle*. The headline read:

Suicide Cult Claims 13 Lives

Bill scanned the article beneath.

"Moorend House at the troubled Queens Park Flats was cordoned off by police today after the discovery of thirteen bodies locked inside one of its apartments. A spokesman for the police refused to confirm reports that all of the deceased had cuts on their arms or whether the deaths are believed to have been the result of a mass suicide pact. There have been allegations that most of the dead were members of a religious cult founded by local businessman and entrepreneur Conrad Chambers. Chambers held a series of controversial meetings in Edgebottom earlier this year, which were condemned by most church leaders in the area because of the unorthodox beliefs expressed at them. All of the remaining residents in Moorend House have been rehoused elsewhere while police carry out their investigations."

"That was here," the little man said.

"It says Moorend House." Bill said. "But I thought - "

"You thought wrong. Whoever sent you here had a vindictive sense of humour. Only dossers like me would choose to come here. And only then because we didn't know any better."

"But the caretaker?"

"Was Chambers. Hadn't you guessed that already?"

"Where you here when all that happened?" Bill asked.

The little man shrugged. It was a very Gallic shrug, though he probably didn't realise it. "I came here after the building was closed. I didn't realise what had happened. I don't come from around here. I didn't know any better. Otherwise I'd have never dared. That was months ago. I think. With all the shit I take I can't hardly remember most of the time. Time gets fuzzy. A few weeks. A few months. A few years. I don't fuckin' know."

Bill guessed that his uncertainty worried him. As well it should, Bill thought. Especially if anything of what he'd seen in this place was true. He still hoped much of it was just imagination. If it were, he wouldn't need to feel guilty about deserting his friends. Though he knew there was nothing he could have done, that if Wayne couldn't handle whatever was down there he would have been even more useless, this didn't help Bill feel any better about himself. After all, he thought remorsefully, they had come here to help him. And all he had done was turn tail and run as soon as things went wrong.

"What did Chambers hope to gain?" Bill asked.

Again the little man shrugged. "Perhaps he had no choice. Perhaps something already here made him. Used him. Like it's using us. Perhaps it's these fuckin' flats."

Bill stared at the junkie worriedly. Was he about to change again? Become that gibbering, grotesque creature that had bounded across this room only minutes ago?

"Don't you want to escape?" Bill asked, hoping to keep the man's mind concentrated. To stop him from becoming something else.

"Escape?" The little man laughed bitterly. "There's only one way to escape – and that doesn't work, not all of the time, believe me." He turned his head towards the small tin box by the window.

A sudden scratching at the door made both of them jolt.

The junkie struck a nicotine-stained finger to his lips. But Bill had no intention of making a sound anyway.

He heard Tracey's voice.

"Bill, let me in. *Please let me in.* I need help."

"Don't do it!" the junkie whispered urgently, a look of terror on his face. He reached out, grasped Bill's arm and added: "It's not her."

Bill irritably tugged his arm from the junkie's fingers. He half rose, undecided. He knew that it probably wasn't Tracey. *He knew this.* After all that had happened he had learnt better than to take anything at face value here. The transformations of the man he was with had taught him that. He wasn't stupid. But the voice was so distinctively Tracey's. And she needed his help. Help which he couldn't keep holding back from her. Not after how he had deserted her and Wayne in the stairwell.

Bill backed away from the junkie, ignored his urgent hand signals to sit down again, and moved towards the door, half tempted to open it, despite what he feared to see outside.

He heard Tracey sob. She banged at the door. Urgently. Pleadingly.

"Bill, please help me. *Please!*"

Unable to ignore Tracey's pleas any longer, Bill grabbed the door handle. He sobbed in fear as he reached for the Yale lock and turned it. The junkie made a last-minute attempt to pull him away, but Bill managed to shrug him off, then whipped the door open. Tracey fell onto him. Blood covered her clothes, and she looked as if she had been cut or ripped about the arms and shoulders. Her hands were drenched with so much blood it dripped from her fingertips.

"They've killed him," she stuttered as she clung on to Bill. "They tore him to pieces."

"Who did?" Bill felt his arms and legs start to shake again and he had an overwhelming need for alcohol. He could almost taste whisky on the tip of his tongue. "Who killed him, Tracey?" He pulled her into the room, then kicked the door shut behind him. The junkie hurriedly locked it again while Bill half carried, half guided Tracey to the settee. Trails of blood stained the floor behind her. And Bill knew she needed to be taken to hospital as soon as possible. Her face looked wretched. Stained with a mixture of tears and blood, her eyes stared into his with a look of hysteria and blind panic.

"There were dogs. Wild dogs. Horrible, ugly pit bulls, Bill. But worse. Much worse."

"Pit bulls?"

"I've seen them," the little man interjected. "They roam here sometimes. In packs," he added, with a shudder. "Nearly caught me once, the bastards did."

"Who owns them?"

The junkie laughed harshly. "If anything their owners are even worse. You must have seen 'em. Sometimes they look normal. Other times they look like they ought to be buried."

"There are a few people like that here," Bill said pointedly, though the junkie didn't seem to notice.

Bill returned to the door. He pressed one ear to it, though his heartbeats were pounding so loudly it was almost impossible to tell if anyone was moving out there. Even so, however frightened he might be, he knew they couldn't remain in the junkie's flat. It might offer them some sort of protection now, but it was no better than a prison. They had to be able to get out of here and out of the flats and back to the real world, he knew, at the same time wishing he had thought to bring a bottle of whisky with him. Or anything that would help to numb his fear.

"What are you going to do?" the junkie asked.

Bill looked at him.

"Have you any knives in your kitchen?"

"Knives?"

"You heard me. Knives. A hammer. Anything that could be

167

used as a weapon. To defend ourselves with."

"I've nothing like that. All I've got is what you see in this room."

Bill gritted his teeth in exasperation. What else should he have expected from the pathetic little drug addict? He looked again at Tracey. She had begun to slump on the settee. The pools of blood beneath it were still growing, and he knew that she needed help as soon as possible if she was going to pull through. Her wounds looked bad, and her face looked even paler now.

Bill returned to the door. If only he knew what was out there. Even though he couldn't see anything through the spyhole, this meant nothing. Its area of visibility was too small. And he knew there could be anything beyond it. Anything at all.

"Don't," the junkie warned, but his voice held little hope that he could dissuade Bill, who had already, suddenly made up his mind. If he didn't act now his doubts and fears would build up again.

Bill grasped the door handle and suddenly turned it.

He stepped out onto the corridor so quickly the whole thing felt totally unreal. The door was violently tugged from his grasp and slammed behind him by the junkie, who just as quickly fastened its locks.

Bill's breath came rapidly as he stood on the corridor, relieved to see that it was empty, despite the sounds of movement from the stairwell. Ignoring these, he hurried to his flat. As soon as he was safely inside, he went to the kitchen where he gathered together a handful of the largest knives he could find amongst the odds and ends of cutlery he had brought with him. At least with something to defend himself with he could make an attempt at getting Tracey out of this place.

What else was there?

His eyes lit on a nearly full bottle of whisky laid on the floor by his bed. He had forgotten about it, though he knew he had reserves like this scattered all about his flat. He took a long, much needed swallow from it, then put the bottle in one of the pockets of his coat, along with most of the knives. He kept one of them, an old, well-sharpened carving knife, in his hand. Ten inches long, its blade was reassuringly heavy.

Bill returned to the corridor. There were still sounds of movement at the far end through the doors to the stairwell, where the lights flickered as if the electrical wiring was coming loose.

"Let me in," Bill whispered urgently as he knocked on the junkie's door.

There was no response. After a minute, Bill knocked again, louder this time.

"Hurry up, for God's sake!"

Still getting no answer, he tried the handle. And was surprised to find that the door wasn't even locked anymore.

Nervously, he stepped inside. The room was darker now, lit only by the moon. Even in the gloom he could see that Tracey was no longer sat on the settee. Instead, curled up on the carpet beneath the window, lay the junkie's corpse. His dried-up face stared sightlessly at him.

Bill backed away from him. The room reeked overpoweringly of death and decay, of mustiness and drugs.

Bill choked back a whimper. How much of all this was real anymore?

His back to the edge of the door, he looked again down the corridor. He had to get out of here. He had no choice.

"But you have."

Bill froze. He recognised the voice, though he had only heard it once before.

He looked towards his flat. Stood in the same shapeless suit he was wearing before, the caretaker looked larger, more imposing than in the lobby. Bill disliked the bland intensity of his eyes.

"I want to leave here," Bill said.

"Of course you do."

Bill's hand tightened about the wooden hilt of the knife.

The caretaker's eyes glanced fleetingly at it, and Bill was sure there was a glimmer of something that might have been either amusement or contempt.

Or both.

Bill turned. He ran down the corridor to the doors at the end, slamming them open with the palms of his hands. One of the wall lights crackled loudly and there was a smell of burnt metal as it flickered, then died, making the area even gloomier than before. The lift doors were open. Inside stood the blank-faced man he'd seen before. Like before, a dark liquid trickled across the floor from about his trainers as he stared at Bill with eyes the colour of rotten eggs. Bill considered the knife in his hand, but somehow it no longer seemed adequate. He contemplated going in the lift with the man, but he knew there was no way he could make himself do that. Instead, he ran towards the stairwell. So far it looked empty. But there were too many sounds of movement below for him to have any illusions about it being empty for long.

The aches in his legs forgotten now, he ran down the stairs with more speed than he'd used in years. He knew this was something he could not sustain. Already his dizziness was getting worse and it was only the momentum of his descent that was keeping him on his feet most of the time. At each turn he had to cling onto the banister rail to stop himself from falling. With the knife in one hand, this was trickier each time he did it, especially when sweat made his palms slippery.

Four flights down and he saw the carnage.

Was this where Wayne had been attacked?

If, he added to himself, his friend and Tracey had ever even come to this place.

Panting heavily, he stared at the bloodied shreds of material scattered across the landing. It looked as if someone had not only been mauled by dogs but almost literally torn to pieces. Some of the piles of rags looked as if there might even be lumps of flesh hidden inside them.

Gagging with disgust, Bill hurried on past. The closer he got to the ground floor he knew there would be more chance to escape. There were still at least six more flights to go. Too many, he knew, to relax.

Tracey's voice halted him.

She was stood on the landing by the torn clothing. Leant against one wall, her own clothes were just as drenched in blood as when he last saw her.

"Where have you been? How did you get here?" He retraced the half dozen steps he'd taken.

"He won't let you go," Tracey said. "He wants you. The whole place wants you."

With a feeling of nausea, Bill knew that she couldn't be real. That she had never even been here today. Neither she nor Wayne. It had all been a trick.

Bill turned away from her and, ignoring whatever she called out to him, raced downstairs with even greater determination.

He started to count each floor he passed. But by the time he'd reached what should have been the ground floor, he was disturbed to see that it blatantly wasn't, that there were still more flights of stairs ahead of him. Could he have miscounted? That would have been easy enough given the circumstances. But, after two more flights and still no sign of the lobby, he knew there was something wrong. What windows he passed showed pitch-black emptiness outside, with no indication of how high he was. After two more floors, he knew he should have reached ground level. Yet still the stairwell continued downwards.

He looked up the stairs. There was someone there, just out of sight. Bill tightened his grip on the knife, though his legs felt weak from all the running he'd done. He reached one hand inside his coat for the bottle of whisky. Unscrewing its lid between his teeth, he spat it out onto the floor, then took a long, hard swallow.

He'd needed that.

He'd been too sober too long, he knew.

And, with a sigh, he took a longer drink.

"You are welcome here."

Conrad Chambers stepped into view. He whistled softly and Bill heard a mad scampering of feet from further down the stairwell.

Dogs' feet, he realised.

Bill listened to them with horror, then held the bottle above his head. Its contents spilled over him, drenching his hair. There had still been nearly two thirds of a litre in the bottle. It dripped down his coat, filling his nostrils with its heady smell of alcohol. He licked his lips.

Saving a large, last portion, he tipped the bottle to his mouth. He'd need it. He would need it more than he had ever needed it in his life.

"You are being foolish," Chambers said.

Bill looked away from him down the stairwell. He could hear them louder. Only seconds later the first of the ugly, deformed brutes looked round the bend in the stairwell at him, its overbite dripping strings of saliva.

His hands shaking, Bill felt inside his coat for his cigarette lighter. What he was going to do terrified him, but it was better than what he knew would happen if he did nothing.

He held the lighter for a moment before his whisky-drenched face as the dog pack started to climb towards him. Powered by button cell batteries, the lighter was exceptionally reliable. It had never failed yet.

But it failed him now.

Three times he tried it. Even a last minute frantic fourth attempt failed to solicit even so much as a spark from the thing.

Bill stared in panic as the grotesque pit bulls edged towards him. He heard Chambers' laugh of mockery. Then watched in horror as the pack surged forwards.

For a moment Bill tried to ward them off with the knife, but there were far too many. They overwhelmed him. Nor were they bothered by the wounds he was able to inflict on them. Almost instantly his wrist was seized between a pair of powerful jaws that remorselessly ground, then broke his bones between razor-sharp fangs and jagged molars the size of oysters. His flesh was shredded into tatters between them. Screaming in agony as the rest of the dog pack ripped and tore and bit at him, Bill tried to fight back. But it was a useless one-sided battle. Blood and flesh, cloth and bones, even the leather from his shoes were ripped and strewn about the stairs as he tried to scramble free. Half blinded by blood, Bill somehow managed to reach the landing, where he had wild hopes of escape through the doors into the corridor, but the powerfully muscled dogs relentlessly dragged him back to the floor. He felt helpless beneath their wild ferocity. A huge, black-faced brute, with pointed, chewed-up ears, transfixed its teeth into his shoulder. It shook him from side to side as if it was trying to rip the flesh from his bones. When he attempted to push himself to his feet, his hands, already missing several fingers, slipped on his blood, and he skidded beneath the dogs, which renewed their attack with even more vigour.

The pain and terror seemed to go on for hours when he finally heard the caretaker's high-pitched whistle. Growling deep inside their massive chests, the dogs reluctantly drew back from Bill, some of them chewing on scraps of flesh still gripped between their teeth.

Through a haze Bill looked up from the ground as Chambers reached down for him. His grey, pulpy, dead man's fingers grasped hold of Bill's collar, and he felt himself being dragged along the floor towards the doors into the corridor. Neon lights flickered noisily overhead with sharp hisses and pops as he was hauled between them.

When he saw the knife in the caretaker's hand Bill knew that his ghastly visions were coming true. Unable to restrain himself, he shrieked for help. But his shouts and screams reverberated along the corridor, echoing and dimming through the endless depths of the stairwell unheard. Chambers, his body monstrously huge and all but shapeless in the growing darkness, loomed above Bill, the carving knife raised high above his head.

For the first few blows that rained down on him Bill's screams continued.

But not for long. And in their place came the *chunk-chunk, chunk-chunk* of a blade hitting meat.

On and on and on...

Twelve months later explosives were laid about the foundations of Moorend House. After years of scandal and endless debates in the council chambers, one of the area's last bastions of Sixties' architecture was about to be demolished. Notorious for years as a haven for drug dealers and addicts, suicides and murders, and more atrocities than most of the rest of Edgebottom had seen in over a century, there were few who would mourn its passing.

Larger crowds than expected had gathered for the spectacle, including newsmen and crews from most of the major broadcasters. There was even a well-known anchorman from BBC North West.

Feeling almost lowly amongst such exalted company as a mere photographer from *The Chronicle*, Paddy O'Shea panned the high-powered telescopic lens of his camera across the tower block. He whistled to himself contentedly, knowing that he was going to get some genuinely dramatic, prize-winning shots today. For once the weather was absolutely bloody perfect. Just the right amount of light and shade, with loads of nice, artistic contrasts. Topping this, he had one of the best positions to view the event from, well above most of the others, on the slopes near the park.

Paddy smiled to himself as he concentrated on zeroing in for a few close ups of the building before it was destroyed.

Which was when something odd caught his eye.

"Two minutes to go," Des Chapel, the reporter who'd been sent to accompanying him, whispered unnecessarily in his ear as a siren began to sound its warning. And, although Paddy should have been readying himself now for a shot of the demolition, his fingers remained still. Almost mesmerised with incredulity, the photographer could not believe what he saw through the lens. Despite the dazzling bursts of sunlight that reflected off some of the windows he was sure there was someone inside the building. This was impossible, he knew. Or should have been. The police were supposed to have searched the flats to make sure they were empty, then sealed them up. Besides, no one in their right mind would want to sneak in there, not when it was about to be reduced to rubble.

Incredulous, Paddy tried to focus more clearly on the tenth-floor windows. He could have sworn a thin faced man with hollow eyes had looked out of one of them. Even more incredibly, there was another man too, he was sure. One window along. Plumper. Taller. Staring with a mournful, frightened expression on his face.

Finally convinced it was not just a trick of the light, Paddy started to shout a warning when the explosions began. Immediately the tall tower block gave a massive, almost slow-motion shrug, as if the whole monolithic building had turned in those instants into an ancient, weather-worn giant. Panic-stricken, birds took to the air in flocks all around the area, while a cloying mixture of brick dust, plaster and shattered concrete erupted across the slopes as the building began its collapse.

Paddy barely noticed any of this. Engrossed, he made his camera follow the window he was watching as it slid with increasing, devastating speed towards the earth, till it finally disappeared amongst the dust and debris that swelled to meet it, unable to take his eye off the face behind it.

Only after he had developed the last few pictures he snapped that day did he realise where he had seen the man before.

Bill Whitley had been on his way out of court two years ago, disgraced and jobless, having been found guilty of assaulting one of his pupils at the school he'd been teaching. Paddy's photograph had dominated the front page of *The Chronicle* the following day.

How the hell did you end up there, Paddy wondered as he stared at the pictures he'd taken, *how the hell did you end up there?*

Also available from
Parallel Universe Publications

BLACK CEREMONIES
by Charles Black
ISBN-10: 0957453558

THE HEAVEN MAKER AND OTHER GRUESOME TALES
by Craig Herbertson
ISBN-10: 0957453517

GOBLIN MIRE
by David A. Riley
ISBN-10: 095745354X

THINGS THAT GO BUMP IN THE NIGHT:
A TREASURY OF CLASSIC WEIRD
edited by Douglas Draa and David A. Riley
ISBN-10: 0957453566

HIS OWN MAD DEMONS:
DARK TALES FROM DAVID A. RILEY
ISBN: 978-0-9574535-8-6

THEIR CRAMPED DARK WORLD AND OTHER TALES
by David A. Riley
ISBN: 978-0-9574535-9-3

Check our website:
http://paralleluniversepublications.blogspot.co.uk/

www.ingramcontent.com/pod-product-compliance
Lightning Source LLC
Chambersburg PA
CBHW070032260626
47159CB00005B/2021